Indie Bites

Ghosts & Guilds

Issue 5: February 2022

A note on language

We are a UK publication, but we accept work from authors all over the world. We retain each author's version of English as written, so pieces from US authors appear in US English and pieces from UK authors appear in British English etc.

Published under licence by Silver Sun Books.

Table of Contents

Letter from the Editor

This quarter's issue is all about ghosts and guilds. The stories we're featuring contain a passel of both, and ask what in the world of the living could be important enough to bring someone back from the dead.

The ghosts you'll meet in these pages run the gamut from friendly faces and old echoes to spectres that are downright terrifying, but what ties them all together is the fact that they are memories: memories of loves lost, of wrongs unavenged and tasks left unfinished. In that sense, they are all about putting things right, tidying away the stray threads of past hurts until natural justice functions as we think it should. In the world of ghosts, grudges are never forgotten and comeuppances – though sometimes a little delayed – are never escaped.

Although you might traditionally associate ghost stories with Halloween, February feels like a month for hauntings to me. It's in that awful sink at the beginning of the year where the joy of Christmas is but a distant memory and spring still feels an age away. It's an easy place for people to get lost, and for bad things to happen. I think that's reflected in our stories, some of which are chilling enough that they demand a warm fire and a hot chocolate or, failing that, a warm pet and a blanket. But a couple of our stories aim to counteract the chill, being so gorgeously light-hearted that they'll make you feel as though you're wrapped up cosy and warm in any circumstances, even if the weather outside is grey and grim. Whatever your preference, we're sure there's at least one story in here that you will love.

We're also bringing you an interview with ghostly hybrid author Arden Powell and three reviews of indie novels from our review team, all on the theme of *Ghosts & Guilds*.

So let's get spooky. There's plenty here to sink your teeth into.

Josie Jaffrey
Anthology Editor

Next month's issue is *Monsters & Masquerades*, and submissions are open now. If you're an indie author, book blogger, illustrator or voice actor who'd like to contribute to one of our upcoming issues, then check out our submissions page on our website. We'd love to have you on board.

A note on language: We are a UK publication, but we accept work from authors all over the world. We retain each author's version of English as written, so pieces from US authors appear in US English and pieces from UK authors appear in British English etc.

Meet Author Arden Powell

Arden Powell is a speculative-fiction author and illustrator from the Canadian East Coast. They graduated from St. Francis Xavier University in 2013 with a Bachelor of Arts degree, Honouring in English Literature. A hybrid author, their first novel, *A Summer Soundtrack for Falling in Love*, was published in 2018 by Riptide Publishing. In 2020 they self-published *The Faerie Hounds of York*, followed by *The Bayou* and *The Bachelor's Valet* in 2021.

When not writing, they can be found drawing, walking the dog, or tending to their exorbitant number of houseplants. They write across multiple sub-genres and everything they write is queer. They can also be found on Twitter (@ArdenPowell).

Welcome to Indie Bites! This quarter we're all about ghosts and guilds, so let's start off with the spectres – tell us a little about your most ghostly book!

My most ghostly book, *The Bayou*, takes place in small-town Louisiana, 1935.

When Eugene was twelve, a girl from town disappeared. Everyone said the gators must have got her when she strayed too near the bayou. No foul play, just a terrible accident. But Eugene can't shake the conviction that Mary Beth's death had something to do with the man who used to haunt her – the man no one else could see.

Now, nearly two decades later, there are more dangerous things than gators in Chanlarivyè. People are disappearing again, and this time, no one can find the bodies. As the town's unease grows, charismatic fugitive Johnny Walker arrives on the scene, shedding bullet casings and stolen bank notes in his wake.

He tangles himself up in Eugene's life and awakens memories Eugene thought he had laid to rest years ago. Memories of the mysterious man who followed Eugene into his dreams, and memories of the bayou – and of the horrifying entity that lurks beneath the water's surface, slowly seeping into the town like a stain.

Without getting into any spoilers, there are two

main ghosts in *The Bayou*. The first is Eugene's memory of Mary Beth, whose death, if she was murdered, remains unsolved and unavenged. The second is the spectre of the man who used to haunt her and Eugene when they played together in the church courtyard as children. Whether that man is a literal ghost or something else altogether remains to be seen.

For me, ghosts evoke sadness rather than horror. I'm not interested in exorcising the ghost to move it along; I want to address the reason it exists in the first place, because usually, that reason – the event that caused the ghost to come into being – is where the horror lies. And that's what *The Bayou* explores.

If you were thrust into a fantasy world, what kind of guild do you think you'd join?

I would love to join an artist's guild! I would apprentice to some master painter or sculptor and live off the favours of my very rich patrons who would all indulge me as I painted nothing but fancy horses for the rest of my life. (Yes, I have put thought into this, and yes, I have spent quite a bit of time drawing fancy horses already. I have yet to write a book that needs a fancy horse on the cover, but it's only a matter of time.)

You write in several very different sub-genres, and traditionally published your first book – do you find self-publishing gives you the freedom to shift between styles more easily? Why did you make the switch to hybrid?

I want to write in as many different genres and sub-genres as possible, and self-publishing allows me to follow my whims without giving an in-house marketing team an aneurism every time I change course. Maybe it would have been smarter to use a different pen name for, say, my horror compared to my romance, but I want to build an author brand that has QUEER SPECULATIVE FICTION as an umbrella term encompassing everything from horror to secondary-world fantasy to fluffy romance without surprising readers. That's the goal.

That said, while I enjoy the complete control self-publishing gives me, I do intend to go the traditional route again when I have the right book for it. There are benefits to both self- and traditional publishing, and I'm interested in exploring all of them. I've also published short stories in literary magazines and small press anthologies, which keeps me active in the traditional-publishing sphere until I have another novel to query.

What does your typical publishing process look like?

I drafted *The Bayou* very quickly back in 2017 or 2018 in response to an open call from one of my favourite publishers. It went through a too-brief round of revisions and then sat in the slush pile for almost two years. By then it was 2020, I had just tested the self-publishing waters with *The Faerie Hounds of York*, and no one had responded to my gentle nudge when I asked for an update about where I stood in the submission queue.

The Bayou was too short to have much hope of getting an agent, and after two years of improving my craft, I no longer thought it was representative of my best work anyway. Rather than wait for it to get rejected, I pulled it from the queue and started serious revisions. The pacing was uneven and too slow, and the ending lacked the kick I wanted it to deliver. I did a lot of cutting up and rearranging of sections to improve the pacing, and added new scenes to increase the horror elements and really push the atmosphere to that creepy, unsettling place I wanted the story to inhabit. I wouldn't have been able to see the structural problems with a clear eye without letting it sit for those two years. It's much easier to kill your darlings when you have some distance from them.

After revisions, the process for most of my books is very similar. I do my own formatting and cover art, and once that's done, I basically boot the book out into the world like kicking a fledgling out of the nest so it can learn to fly. The actual publishing of the book is kind of chaotic – I don't have a marketing team and I mostly rely on my tiny cluster of loyal readers (whom I love and cherish) to hype it up naturally. Which has worked surprisingly well for me so far! Maybe one day I'll pin down a really concrete publishing strategy and launch my career to the next level, but right now I feel like one of those street performers playing like ten hundred instruments at once? So we'll see how far that takes me.

What's a ghost story you love?

The Haunting of Tram Car 015 by P. Djèlí Clark! It's a fantasy adventure set in early 1900's Cairo rather than a spooky paranormal type of ghost story, and the ghost in question isn't quite what it seems, but it *is*, as the title declares, a haunting. And it's excellent. Immersive worldbuilding, engaging characters, and the ghost – djinn – spirit – is properly menacing.

Which indie fantasy authors are you enjoying at the moment?

T Kingfisher is one of my favourite writers as well as being ultimate author goals. I love her books, the frequency of her publications, and her eagerness to branch out across different genres. I haven't delved into her recent horror books yet, but I'm looking forward to them next time I want to be delightfully creeped out. Her fantasy romance novels are great if you want something a little lighter but still with a respectable body count. I appreciate a murder or two in a romance.

I'd also like to shout out a couple of my favourite webcomics because they're such a cool branch of the indie scene. *Tiger, Tiger* by Petra Nordlund is a swashbuckling fantasy comic in gorgeous greyscale about a young noblewoman who steals her brother's identity and his ship in order to indulge her preoccupation with sea sponges. And *Kill Six Billion Demons* by Abbadon, a.k.a. Tom Parkinson-Morgan, is a violent, full-colour comic painted in vivid, painstaking detail about a girl transported to a demon realm where she learns that she's some kind of chosen one who needs, as the title suggests, to kill six billion demons. It's insane and amazing.

What's in store for your readers next?

I have a new book that just came out in January!

Winter's Dawn isn't ghostly, but it does have gothic trappings. It's a standalone fantasy novella with a male lead and a nonbinary love interest, which is a character I'm very excited about. It's in Kindle Unlimited and available on Amazon.

Sounds exciting! Thank you so much for joining us!

Short Fiction

Weirdo

Gemma Church

I am not happy. Not happy at all. Trick or treating is my favourite time of year (except Christmas and my birthday) and Mum has said that me and my friends have to take along the new kid, Otis, just because she promised his mum that we would.

Let's get one thing straight.

Otis is a complete weirdo.

He's a good foot taller than everyone else in our class and barely talks to anyone. If he wasn't such a weirdo, he'd probably make a great rugby player, being as wide as he is tall. But he's got one of those extra teaching assistants who has to help him do the simplest stuff. It's embarrassing and means we have to do loads of special stuff for him in class too. It's a complete drag.

Like the other day, when Jenny accidentally dropped the box of paintbrushes on the classroom floor, he completely freaked out. Like, completely. It was like watching my two-year-old brother have a tantrum, but Otis is obviously bigger and was more difficult to pin down when he started screaming and tearing all our artwork off the walls.

Wanna know the worst of it? He didn't even get in trouble. Mrs Owens just let him get away with it and come back into class like nothing had even happened once he'd calmed down. If I'd done anything like that it would have been straight to the headmaster's office for a proper telling off.

And he smells. Otis, not the headmaster. Not bad, like, but his uniform stinks of that *Febreze* spray stuff that people use to hide nasty smells and there's always a whiff of something like gone-off food about him.

Anyway, I told Mum all this and do you know what she said?

"His mum just wants Otis to make some new friends. She'll be there with you on Halloween if Otis can't cope, so you don't need to worry about looking after him, just try to include him, that's all I'm asking."

That's all she's asking? Is she having a laugh? If Craig from Year 12 and his gang see us with Otis and his mum, then we won't hear the end of it. This is a disaster. Beyond a disaster. Social suicide of the highest order.

Otis lives on a crappy estate at the edge of the village, one of those new builds where they "have to include social housing to pacify those lefty idiots," according to Dad.

Anyway, I don't agree with everything Dad says but I can see what he means about them all being poor. There's barely a pumpkin in sight when we trudge down the street, so we'll have to go back to my end of the village to go trick or treating. What a pain. I hope all the good sweets aren't gone by the time we've picked up Otis and his mum, then walked back again.

When we turn up to his front door, there are no lights on inside and I let out a huge sigh of relief, which makes a weird whistling sound through my Storm Trooper helmet.

"Let's just go. I don't think there's anyone in," I say, crossing my fingers behind my back.

"Maybe we should just try the bell?" Jenny says. She's too nice for her own good, Jenny, agreeing to dress up as Rey from Star Wars even though she's not a major fan of the latest films. She's more of a Trekkie or *Empire Strikes Back* sort of girl and (don't tell anyone I said this, but) she's pretty cool for a girl too.

"Nah, Jenny, listen to our man Finn here and let's just go," Mark says, tugging at the belt on his new X-Wing fighter costume. He looks proper boss and I'm a bit jealous. Wish I'd thought of that costume.

But before we have time to ring the bell or leave the little front garden, the door creaks open, like, real slow. It sounds like something from an old black and white horror movie when a vampire appears, all fangs and fake blood, ready to pounce on some sappy girl wearing white. But we're not outside some gothic mansion in Transylvania. We're outside a council house in Cambridgeshire. And instead of Count Dracula, Otis is standing there in the darkness in the lamest ghost outfit I've ever seen. He's just taken a sheet and cut some holes in it, for pity's sake.

"Hi, Otis, is your mum here?" Jenny asks, smiling and stepping forward.

Otis steps back and shakes his head.

"Oh, okay, shall we just go without her then?" she

says.

Otis nods and steps forward, the door closing behind him as quietly as a mouse.

“Nice outfit,” Jenny says, her smile now looking more like rigor mortis. “Did your mum make it?”

Otis just shrugs and marches off. He’s fast, faster than I was expecting, gliding down the street under the glowing orange streetlights like he’s on roller skates. Maybe he is, you can’t tell anything about him under that sheet.

“Be like that then,” I say, a little too loudly. “Shall we just leave him to it?”

“Oi, be nice,” Jenny says, elbowing me hard in the ribs and running after Otis.

Storm Trooper me and X-Fighter Mark are left standing there like a pair of padawan puddings and I’m in half a mind to suggest that we go the opposite way without them. Create our own little trick-or-treat rebellion.

“Come on man,” Mark says. “It could be worse, at least no one will know it’s Otis under that sheet and we can’t exactly leave Jenny on her own with that weirdo.”

I know he’s right and we run after them, our empty pumpkin buckets swinging in our hands.

The night goes pretty well, all things considered. More people in the village seem to be up for a bit of trick or treating this year than last. One of the snooty parish councillors has even got in the proper Halloween spirit (pun intended) and is handing out big bags of sweets from his front door. He’s one house to remember for next year, defo.

To be honest, Otis is no trouble either, he just glides along next to us and doesn't say a word. The only thing that raises a few eyebrows with folk is that he puts his hands over his ears when we shout 'trick or treat' and makes this weird humming sound that he sometimes makes in class too when things get loud. But otherwise, everything goes without a hitch, and I start to feel a bit guilty about kicking up such a fuss about him coming with us. It's a bit like being angry with a puppy. A ghost puppy.

Otis also seems to know where loads of other Halloween-friendly houses are too, even though he only moved here a few weeks ago. He takes the lead, and we follow as he takes us from house to house, down some streets I've never even been to before. Some of them look like dead ends but there's always someone there willing to give us some sweets.

"Top work, Otis," I concede, having to cram candy into my pockets to make room in my bucket for some more. "Wait, mate, where's your bucket?"

But he just stands there, quiet as a grave.

"Haven't you been getting any sweets at the houses we've been going to?"

He shakes his head and I feel this weird ache in my chest.

Jenny steps forward. "Then, we'll share ours with you when we've finished. It's only fair, isn't it? Mark? Finn? After Otis helped us find all those houses with sweets. We never would have found them without you."

She eyeballs me and Mark until we feel the size of

fleas.

We mumble our agreement. To be honest (though I won't admit it out loud) Jenny does have a point. In fact, I'm almost warming to Otis until he leads us across the park, and guess who we run into? That's right. Craig and his gang.

Otis is about the same size as Craig and his gang (put together, they're lanky streaks of piss the lot of them), but I see him shrink into his ghost costume when they swagger up, shouting and howling at the moon like they're werewolves. They've not exactly made much of an effort for Halloween either, each of them just wearing black hoodies and one of those masks from *Scream*.

I feel my palms start to sweat and my knees buckle just a bit. I hope we can slip away before they see us. No such luck.

"What do we have here?" Craig shouts at us. "Princess Leia and her robot idiots?"

Jenny rolls her shoulders back and sticks her chin forward.

"Come on, just ignore them," she says to us, and there's only a slight tremor in her voice as we start to walk past, but Craig steps ahead and blocks the path.

Craig's skinny with mousey hair, buck teeth, and a hooked nose. I sometimes wonder if he decided to be the school bully because otherwise, he'd be the number one target of any other bullies out there. But I don't think I can credit Craig with that much intelligence.

He folds his twiglet arms over his chest and his mates stand behind him, adopting the same pose with their *Scream* masks pushed back over their heads. They look like the world's worst boy band. The name 'Ghouls Aloud' unexpectedly pops into my head. I'd smile if I wasn't so close to shitting myself.

"And who's under the sheet?" Craig shouts, for no reason as we're only centimetres away from him now. His breath stinks of vapes. "Your mum? It's a shame she doesn't put a sheet over her head all year round, she's so butt ugly!"

This poor excuse for a joke gets an over-enthusiastic laugh from Craig's mates, who hit each other in their sides and bend over like jackals.

"Excuse us," Jenny says, trying to push past. It's a valiant effort and, for a moment, I imagine her pulling out her staff and kicking ass like Rey would. But she's only 13 years old and her hands are shaking so much that candy starts to rain from her bucket.

It happens as quick as a blink. One minute, me, Mark and Jenny and Otis are standing there. The next minute, three of us are on the floor and they're trying to pull our buckets from our hands. Mark and me, we give ours away in an instant, but Jenny is as stubborn as she is kind and gets a hard kick in the ribs from Craig.

"No! Leave her alone!" I shout. "You don't hit girls, ever!"

"But I've been beating you up for years, you little pussy," Craig shouts, giving me an identical kick in the ribs. The pain bursts up my side and down my arm like an electric shock and I curl into a ball.

Only Otis is left standing, frozen to the spot. His sheet is quivering as Craig and his friends circle round him, laughing.

"Where's your candy, mate?" Craig sneers. "You hiding it under that shit-stained sheet? Give it over or you'll get a kicking as hard as your mates have."

Otis turns to look at me and, if I didn't know better, I'd swear one of those holes in his sheet just winked at me.

Then, the streetlights in the park go out. I can't make out much in the gloom, but I see Craig and his gang pulling closer around Otis and his sheet being thrown into the air. It looks like a proper ghost now, some sort of spectre hanging there, pendulous in the starless night sky.

I stand up as quickly as I can (which isn't very quick at all, my ribs are still killing me) to run over and help Otis. Poor kid.

"He doesn't have any candy, you leave him alone!" I yell, standing as straight as I can.

But Craig and his mates don't hear me. No one does. Because Craig and his mates are screaming as high and loud as a group of girls at a Harry Styles concert, drowning out my words.

Craig steps back, white as snow, and stumbles to the side, throwing up the cheap cider and stolen sweets he's doubtless been gorging on all night. His gang runs away like a pack of rats. I catch Craig's eye and hold his stare. Now he's the one shaking. "What the…?" he whispers. "What is that?"

"That's our friend Otis, that's who he is. You can do one," I say, trying to smile through the pain.

"Yeah," Jenny says from the floor, slowly getting

up. "And don't think about trying to beat us up or anyone else at school or we'll tell everyone that you and your mates were crying and screaming like a group of little girls on Halloween."

"We'll tell them you pissed yourself too," Mark adds, for good measure, and I feel his hand on my shoulder. "Now, you leave us alone."

Craig's gaze hasn't left mine the whole time, his eyes brimming with tears and his mouth wide open. "You and your mates are fucked-up weirdos," he says, holding up his hands before running off into the night, faster than Usain Bolt with a rocket up his arse.

"Better a weirdo than a pissy-pants idiot!" I shout after him, wishing I'd thought of something more impressive to say in front of Jenny.

The streetlights come back on, and Otis is stood there with the sheet back over his head. We rush over to hug him, but he puts his arms up under the sheet and moves back, shaking his head so violently it's a wonder that sheet doesn't come off.

"It's okay, Otis, we won't come near you," Jenny says, clutching her side. "They didn't hurt you, did they? Are you okay?"

He nods.

"What the hell did you do to them Otis?" I ask. "We couldn't see with them all crowded round you."

Otis just stands there and shrugs.

"Well," Mark says, "I for one don't care what you did or how you did it. Nice work, Otis, mate. You can have all my candy for getting rid of Craig."

"Mine too!" Jenny says, turning to raise her

eyebrow at me.

"Mate, I'll throw in the bucket too," I say. "Come on, let's pick up these sweets and get you home."

Otis nods and I still can't see his face, but I hope he's smiling. The sheet has kind of folded strangely around his mouth to make it look like he's smiling anyway.

Me, Jenny and Mark scamper around the ground and grab all our sweets, picking off blades of grass and bits of mud as we go along. My chest stings and aches in a way that's nothing to do with the beating I just got.

"Otis? Do you want to come back to mine tonight for a bit?" I ask. "Play a bit of Xbox?"

But when I look up, I catch a glimpse of his sheet gliding along the park before disappearing below the horizon.

"Has he gone?" Jenny asks. "We really should make sure he gets home okay."

"Oh, I think he'll be just fine," I say.

The next day at school Craig isn't in, which makes me happy. Really happy. But Otis isn't in either and there's a strange vibe in the classroom. Mrs Owens is all pink-eyed and quiet and Otis and his teaching assistant are nowhere to be seen.

"Do you think he's okay? Otis?" Jenny whispers to me.

I shrug.

"Maybe we should have checked he got home okay last night?"

Before I have a chance to reassure her, Mrs Owens

stands up and starts talking to our class.

I don't fully take in what she says. But I hear the words "Otis" and "happened straight after school" and "no one knows what happened" and "ambulance called" and "his mum took him to the hospital" and "too late".

It's raining outside. I look out of the window and try to block out everything else Mrs Owens is saying. I don't want to hear it because if I hear it, then it's real.

So, I put my hands over my ears and start to hum to block out the noise. I think Jenny takes my hands away from my ears and holds them, but I can't feel it. Everything's such a blur. I wipe the condensation away from the window and focus on the raindrops outside to stop my own tears from falling. My focus relaxes beyond those raindrops and the playground, past the school gates to the park across the way, where I swear I see a lad wearing a sheet, waving at me.

I wave back, but he's already gone.

Gemma Church is a former physicist and current freelance science and technology copywriter with a recent Diploma in Creative Writing at Cambridge University.

Wuthering Sprites

Alice James

"It's hardly surprising that your brother's ghost isn't at rest," Ernest the Exorcist said. He waved his divining crystal around in a cheerful manner at the draughty vestibule with its half-papered walls and boarded-up front window. "I mean no offense, Your Grace, but he was the very prince of procrastination and unfinished projects."

He had a point. Peregrine's ambitious beginnings were so often the victims of his own short attention span. Not that my mother had been any help in that respect. She was always encouraging him to start more and more open-ended restorations. I think she feared that if the manor was ever structurally sound enough to sit down in comfort for ten minutes, without getting rained on, snowed in or attacked by sparrows, that Peregrine might get a social life, or even a girlfriend, and leave home.

In the end of course, she'd died just six months before him, leaving Peregine behind in a twenty-four bedroomed ruined mansion that was so dilapidated and unalluring that none of his debtors could be bothered to foreclose on it. He'd followed her two weeks ago after falling off the roof whilst trying to retile the cupola in a blizzard. I know I always tell people that mother was the crazy one in the family, but Peregrine wasn't all that far behind. I got out young; eloping was the making of me.

I sat down on an embroidered chair that creaked ominously as it released a cloud of dust and the odd moth. Adamant Manor had seen better days, perhaps, but not in my memory.

"Sir, I pray you're wrong," I said. "If his spirit is going to roam these hauls restlessly until they are all spick and span, it has quite the wait ahead of it."

"My dear," Ernest said. He was beginning to forget to be formal with me, which was a relief. He'd always been one of that posse of uncles that families acquire, those ad hoc guests you're not quite sure you are actually related to but who are always around. "My dear, I do hope not. And your family, let's not forget, has rarely been prone to post-death malingering." He patted my hand in a paternal manner. "Now, are you sure you'll be alright on your own here? I can send to the house for an overnight bag and stay here with you if you're uncomfortable, you know."

I blinked. It was a very kind gesture from a man who'd just walked through the entire manor with me and had a very good idea of just how uncomfortable a night spent here would be. This was a place that, in its heyday, would have been a shining jewel in the nation's diadem of gothic glory, a wonder of stained glass and carved granite, the roofs a joyful riot of black slate, gargoyles and ornate curlicues. These days it was tough to decide whether rising damp or dry rot was drawing ahead in the race, and my brother and the servants had established a code of chalk markings on the upper storeys that denoted where the floors were safe to walk on.

"Dear Uncle Ernest," I said, much moved, "I'll hardly be alone, you know. I brought my maid, my majordomo, my groom and two footmen with me to Adamant and, while the household here is very much a skeleton staff, they all knew me as a girl and they are particularly devoted to my comfort." Not least because it transpired that my arrival was the first sign they'd had since my mother died that they might possibly get paid… "Now, shall I call my carriage round for you?"

Ernest bowed very elegantly. He also looked noticeably relieved, however; I didn't think he'd relished the prospect of a night spent within these walls.

"No no, my dear," he said. "I came on Nelly – she does love a winter walk. Now, I'll leave you with this leaflet – it tells you how to divine exactly what kind of ghost Peregrine has become, and that might give us some clues on how to send him on his way."

I waved Ernest off from the porch. My mother's ancient butler Dormid stood to attention next to me, his hunched form still dignified and reassuring, albeit supported at both elbows by two footmen clad in rather moth-eaten uniforms. He'd been a butler here since before I was born and was showing no signs of wanting to retire.

"Will Your Grace take tea?" he asked politely.

"No, not this afternoon," I said hastily. "Why don't you let them know downstairs?"

Ernest had wanted to test each and every room for

spectral emanations and our perambulations had taken us through the sculleries and into the kitchen. Two grooms, an undermaid and the housekeeper were all trying to persuade the oven to light; one of the grooms was already in tears. The thought of what would happen if Dormid told them they had to magic up some cream cakes was too cruel to contemplate.

I made my way back to the library. It was one of the only rooms in the whole house where the fireplace *and* the window embrasures had somehow escaped both the depredations of time and Peregrine's attentions. I poked the fire out of its sluggish torpor, curled up in the least-dusty armchair and took out Ernest's leaflet.

"*All ghosts*," it read, "*can be defined by their motivation, their location boundaries, and their ethereal immanence.*"

He listed pages of diverse motivations, but they did indeed all boil down to unfinished business of some kind, such as revenge, the discovery of buried treasure or the restoration of a family's good name. Location boundaries were also fairly easy. Most commonly, ghosts were tied to a location, and this was known as a haunting. However, they could occasionally be bound to a person, which was termed possession, or an object, which amounted to entity anathema – or, in common parlance, a curse. And within these divisions, Ernest noted that some could only appear at certain times of the day or night or even only on special days such as family christenings or the anniversary of a particular event.

I put down the leaflet and rubbed my eyes. Qualifying as an exorcist was one of the most challenging degrees, requiring seven years of academic study, and I was starting to see why. Only Pendle College Cambridge and Gwen Ellis College Oxford currently offered the course. I knew that Ernest had once upon a time been one of Gwen Ellis's brightest students, winning award after award, but he'd chosen a quiet country parish in which to exercise his talents. It was a blessing; many large towns struggled to attract a decent exorcist, and yet this insignificant rural nowhere could boast one of the finest in the country.

Steeling myself, I picked up the leaflet again and moved on to ethereal immanence: this, it transpired, described the powers or influences of a ghost: visual, oral, emotional or physical. All ghosts possessed one or more of these.

Ghosts that could only be seen were called apparitions, while those you could only hear were known as ghouls. Similarly, spirits you could only feel were termed shades and those that could only effect their physical surroundings were known as poltergeists. However, a ghost could have any combination of these four attributes and that was where things became complicated. Phantoms could be both heard and felt, for example, so you might notice music and a feeling of despair. Sprites, on the other hand, could be seen and also felt. I was pretty sure my brother was a sprite. I'd seen him walking endlessly down the corridors and gained a great sensation of urgency from his appearances, but he'd not seemed able to speak to me or touch anything.

I opened my travelling writing desk and took out a sheet of paper. Trimming my quill, I began some notes for Ernest.

"*I believe that I have identified Peregrine's spirit as being of the type known as a sprite,*" I began. "*He seems bound to the lower levels of Adamant Hall, and I believe his unfinished errand to be one of some urgency.*"

The window rattled and I looked up. I'd spent the past ten days in my former childhood home and I didn't think I'd been warm for a single one of them. The snow, which had been falling half-heartedly since the morning, had finally got its act together and was now coming down in a confetti of thick clumps. The overgrown lawns that led down to the main gates were losing their tussocks and hummocks underneath an eiderdown of white. The deep narrow roads around the estate would very swiftly become impassable. My journey home, had I even hoped to make it soon, would be off the cards for many days to come.

I sighed and got to my feet. If I wanted a breath of fresh air before darkness fell, I had perhaps an hour before sunset. One of my own footmen, Nathaniel, was hovering in the rear hall and as I entered he stood to attention.

"Your Grace," he said and, correctly divining my errand, added: "Let me fetch your coat and boots."

I waited as he hurried away, returning moments later with many soft, warm layers. He knelt down and competently changed my house slippers for tough, lace-up boots. I was fond of Nathaniel. He'd been barely more than a boy when he'd started with us at the town house in London; I'd been barely more than a girl. The duke had picked him out for his charming smile and astoundingly orange curls. I'd kept him on afterwards for his sweetness of manner, his humour and his kindness. A house full of people like Nathaniel would always be a happy house.

I shrugged myself into my fur coat with his help and donned a selection of scarves, a hat and gloves.

"Would you like me to accompany you, Your Grace?" he asked, unbarring the garden door and flinging it open. A flurry of snow blew in, along with a handful of leaves. "Or would you like some peace?"

"Come with me," I replied, stepping into the wind. "You can recount me tales of this strange, bereaved and haunted household."

We walked along the veranda and down into the knot garden, the roses within the low box hedges clipped down to little more than twigs for the winter. At the end it opened into an arbour, the paths beneath the trees still free of snow. A little wind and that wouldn't last, but it was a charming place to walk while keeping my boots dry. In the London house I rarely had time to myself. There was a constant stream of callers, visitors and tradesmen, and endless demands from the staff. The big house was worse. If I stepped outside for an instant, a gardener or gamekeeper would be upon me in moments with supplications or demands for instruction. When the duke had been alive, much of this had fallen to him. Now that there was just me, I often felt myself too thinly spread. Here there were few staff left to bother me. At some point I would have to make a decision about whether to pour countless thousands into the place to bring it up to scratch or abandon it to the elements. I was favouring the latter but mostly because the thought of taking on another estate was daunting.

Nathaniel had clearly been over mulling my request because, as we turned back to the house, he said:

"It's not an unhappy household, Your Grace, considering how it's been falling down around them and they were never ever paid on time. Your mother was very good natured and always made sure they had time to see their families. The doctor was always on call if they were sick and of course your brother was very popular too. And for such an old house, it's relatively ghost-free – there's only really your great, great, great grandfather the admiral, and he's all the way up on the roof."

I laughed.

"I forgot about the admiral. He's the dearest poltergeist and would play ball games with my brother and I for hours on end when we were young. He was terrifyingly good with snowballs! I was up there today, but of course he only comes out at night. I must pop up one evening to pay him my respects."

We turned at the belvedere, which was already wearing a snowy hat, and I skidded a little in the ice. Nathaniel caught my arm and steadied me.

"Thank you," I said. "You know, I seem to remember that, when I was a child here, we also had a ghoul in the wine cellar that was frightfully annoying when one wanted port, but Ernest took care of him for us. Nathaniel, let's walk around the lake to the front door. I love that view of the village from the west side of the house."

"Of course, Your Grace." He gave me a hand up a flight of slippery steps whose banisters had long since been lost to the ravages of Father Time. "Your sojourn here is a great excitement to them. They expected you to leave immediately after the funeral. If you'll pardon me for speaking out of turn, mistress, it's raised their hopes."

His words lingered awkwardly in my mind. A tumbled-down semi-ruin full of miserable people was one thing; a house full of contented staff looking eagerly towards better times was a very different prospect, and one much harder to write off.

"Thank you for your honesty," I said. "Now, who on earth could this be?"

Dormid stood at the front door, waiting to greet the two men who were approaching. They had clearly just dismounted from two fine horses, which were somewhat beladen with bandboxes and trunks. The taller of my unexpected visitors, whose dress proclaimed him to be a valet, had taken both sets of reins and was leading the beasts as the second, dressed warmly in a many-caped riding coat, made his way up the arc of decaying stone steps to the entrance way.

The butler cast me a look of enquiry, and I nodded, letting Nathaniel help me up the stairs. The man turned at my approach and revealed a handsome, swarthy countenance that spoke of many years in hotter sun than was to be found in the green and pleasant land of England. His eyes were a bright and piercing green, and long dark curls were making their way out from under a warm woollen hat. He looked vaguely familiar, but I couldn't place him.

He started visibly at seeing me.

"Your Grace," he said. "I had no expectation that you would be here. This is a singular honour. Forgive my tardy arrival – your brother must be wondering whether I had fallen victim to footpads – but the weather made our journey all but impossible, and we abandoned my coach some three hours back."

I curtseyed slightly and held out a hand, which he took and kissed in the formal manner.

"I fear your errand is untimely," I said. "Peregine died two weeks ago. But please, come out of the cold and my men will stable your horses and welcome your valet. Whatever invitations my brother extended to you it is my pleasure to endorse."

I wasn't sure how close he'd been to my brother and, if my words caused him grief, I didn't want to embarrass the man, so I walked ahead of him into the house. I took my time unbuttoning my coat to give him any privacy that was needed, but it appeared that none was. He bounded into the hallway after me and pressed his fingers to his temples.

"Your Grace, I never met your brother, but our correspondence was over a quite extraordinary matter and, if his death was unexpected and he did not confide its nature to anyone other than myself, then I fear we have no time at all to lose," he said in tones of great agitation.

I shook my head, confused.

"Peregine's death was a sudden accident," I said. "But I have no notion of what you speak. He confided in no one about anything – it was not his way."

He flung out his hands in a manner that was almost wild.

"He told you nothing about this?" he asked, his voice rising. "He did not mention the astounding family secret that he had found buried here?"

I took a step backwards, a little startled at his intensity.

"Sir, be calm," I said as gently as I could manage. "I have not spoken to my brother in nearly twenty years. He has confided nothing in me since he broke a ceramic bust of one of our uglier ancestors whilst practicing his bowling in the orangery when he was meant to be studying his history primer." My words caused my unnamed guest to smile, and some of the stress left his shoulders. "Panic not," I added. "Whatever is urgent we shall address. Now, please join me in the library – it's the only warm room in the house bar the kitchen – and my staff will bring you some hot tea and toast while you tell me your tale."

"My name," my visitor began, "is Sir Lancelyn Coeur de Lyon. I can see that you do not recall me, but I saw you many times at college dinners. I was a student of your husband's at Gwen Ellis."

I clapped my hands together.

"You have no idea what a delight it is to meet a student of Lamb's," I said. "I miss him so. It's been two years now, but…" I trailed off before gathering myself together. "But one always misses those who are taken too soon," I finished more formally.

We'd met when I was just seventeen. I was a gawky schoolgirl whose mother planned for her to marry money. He was twice my age, the impoverished third son of a duke. We'd eloped and she never spoke to me again, not even when his two brothers were tragically killed in the war, his father died of grief and I became the wealthy duchess of Lambton before my twentieth birthday. Peregine, ever under her thumb, hadn't tried to mend the rift. I bore them no ill will – they were, after all, both dead and my life had been a very happy one.

My guest pressed his hands together in sympathy.

"Indeed," he said. "Before he inherited the title, your husband was the foremost expert in the country on dragons and basilisks, and it was a great privilege to have him as my tutor. I don't claim any such prestige, but I published a small volume on the demise of the golden dragon two years ago, and I believe that is how your brother came to reach out to me."

I felt my eyes widen.

"Golden dragons are extinct, though, are they not, Sir?"

"Not quite," he said. "His Majesty keeps the very last known male dragon in the gardens at Windsor Castle. Alas, Archibald is believed to be the last of his kind."

Now that he mentioned it, I remembered. Lamb had

told me that the golden dragons were the sweetest-natured and most loyal of all the breeds. They had never been numerous, coming from a single mountain top in Snowdonia, and had been slaughtered almost entirely in the war due to mismanagement by the vice admiral of Nelson's flying corps. The king had offered a fifty-thousand-pound reward for a female of the species to breed with lonely Archibald, but no one had ever claimed it.

"I see," I said. "But Peregine never had the slightest interest in dragons that I was aware of."

"I think that changed very suddenly," Lancelyn said. "Two months ago, he wrote to me out of the blue. He said that in a hidden cellar of this house he had found a sea chest containing a great egg and believed it to be that of a golden dragon. I have been corresponding with him on the best way to bring it to hatch – and I believe it is due to emerge this very evening."

I felt my mouth fall open in surprise. While Lamb had been alive, our home had always been full of infant dragons and baby basilisks. The eggs would remain dormant for many decades if locked up in a cold dark place but, brought into the moonlight, they would begin to develop. On the next full moon, the egg should be placed on a brazier at midnight. And at that point you needed to make sure you had plenty of sulphur and raw chicken to hand, because the dear creatures emerged quite ravenous...

"In that case, if Peregine has been exposing the egg to moonlight, you are quite right," I said. "We need to set up a brazier on the roof without delay. Raw meat I can certainly demand from the kitchen, but sulphur might be harder."

"I brought plenty," he said. "I don't know, however, where your brother was keeping the egg. He said it was in a secret place that no stranger could ever find."

"Ah," I said. "In that case I know exactly where it is. There's an enchanted chamber inside the cupola that can only be opened by the heir or head of the family. I suppose that, right now, I am the only person who could possibly access it."

I glanced across at the clock. It was already three, and the light would soon begin to fade. I felt that I had a long, dark evening up on a wintry roof ahead of me.

"We should begin immediately," I said. "I can't tell you how many times the Lamb assured me we'd have a hatchling with us before supper and we were still feeding coals into the fire at dawn."

I'd forgotten how delightful it feels to open a secret way that is only yours. The stone wall of the lichen-pocked cupola turned oak brown as I placed my hand on it, revealing the enchanted door, and the handle opened without the need of a conventional lock. Inside was neat and dust free, papers and an empty tea cup lined up in an orderly fashion – my brother had clearly made this his personal space for many years.

The egg was a curiously orange colour, quite different from anything I'd seen before. It sat on a cushion in front of the cupola windows, where it would have received plenty of moonlight in the past month, and it had the crackleware finish of a shell just ready to hatch. Our task was truly urgent! The sky was almost dark by the time Lancelyn, Nathaniel and I had our hastily constructed brazier lit on the flat part of the roof; I'd adapted the mesh from a unwanted rose bowl to hold the fire, and a discombobulated cook had sent up a china bowl of sausage meat.

"We should probably watch in shifts," I said, adding a fresh coal to the flames and placing the egg carefully on top. "There's no telling when it will emerge."

"Indeed," Lancelyn said, poking the fire with the mighty poker that he had liberated from the Great Hall fireplace.

Something in his voice unnerved me, but I couldn't place it. I looked up at him, but he was regarding the egg, which was already glowing slightly red. For an instant, his expression was one of unmasked greed… but then it was gone.

"I will watch first, if you wish," he said pleasantly, his expression back to its usual humility. "You could perhaps take a light supper?"

"Yes, of course," I said, hoping my voice sounded calm. "Nathaniel, could you kindly help me to collect my things from the cupola."

I hurried inside and tried to catch my breath. What did I know of Lancelyn apart from the fact that he claimed acquaintance with my brother – and had coaxed me to reveal a hidden prize worth a bounty of fifty thousand pounds! Just in case he should be watching me, I made a show of gathering up our accoutrements. His pot of sulphur stood on a side table.

It had been wrapped in a sheet of *The Times*, which I was about to crumple when I saw what story was on the page. My heart leapt in fear.

"Nathaniel," I whispered. "This is Peregine's obituary. Lancelyn said he didn't know my brother was dead – but that was a lie."

He hurried over to me and leant over the table.

"Your Grace," he began.

But I had realised our danger all too late. Before he could finish his sentence, a shadow loomed at the door, a raised arm whistled down and Nathaniel dropped like a stone. I screamed in horror. Lancelyn had clubbed him down with the poker.

"No," I said. I dropped to my knees. Nathaniel lay as though dead; there was blood in his red hair. "Nathaniel, speak to me." I felt tears running down my cheeks. I looked up at Lancelyn as he stood above me. "How could you? He is my oldest friend – he is all I have left. Please; you can have the egg, and the money. Just let me summon a doctor."

He laughed.

"You think I'd be happy with a gift of fifty thousand pounds from our foppish king when the French will pay me three times that? They have a male dragon in the dungeons at Versailles." He reached down and seized me by my collar. "I don't suppose anyone will be surprised that a lonely widow flung herself to her death at the site of her brother's demise, eh? Your Peregrine made such a fuss when I pushed him off – will you scream as much?"

I tried to resist him, but my feet slid on the icy

stone. With the setting of the sun, the roof had frozen to an icy death trap; I just hadn't thought it was my death that would transpire. Snow was falling in thick armfuls. I felt it patinate my face.

"Please," I said, and he dragged me towards the edge of the roof. "You don't have to do this." My voice was lost in the growing wind of the storm. "There are other ways."

Just as we reached the very edge of the roof, my feet slipped from under me and I fell onto my face, biting my tongue. Lancelyn lost his grip on me and gave a grunt of impatience. I looked up at him, the taste of blood in my mouth but, just as he began to reach down to haul me up, he was struck in the face by a snowball.

"What the..." he began before another hit him full on. And another. And then another. The admiral had clearly arisen for his wintry night of haunting and he had lost none of his cricketing skills. A hail of white struck Lancelyn, dozens of snowballs one after the other smacking into his face and torso. Losing his balance for a moment, he took a step backwards... There wasn't a sound above the howl of the wind as he toppled off the edge of the roof and plummeted through some seventy feet of dark night air to the stone courtyard below.

When the Lamb died, I never envisaged another moment of contentment, but fate – ever the scamp – loves to spring surprises, and indeed I have so much joy in my life now that I sometimes find myself dizzy with it. I have not forgotten my first love – does one ever? – but my memories are no longer tinged with despair. I know he would want only my happiness.

The ton reacted with their usual mixture of vicarious disgust and glee to the news that the Duchess of Lambton had married her footman, but I sense equal amounts of jealousy in the mix. By the time we emerge from the countryside, I expect it will all be long forgotten and they will have moved on to the next scandal.

But in truth, it may take some time. Lancelyn's treatise on the golden dragon was adamant on how damaging it can be to relocate the hatchlings in their first few years, so we are stranded here for the foreseeable future. I do not mind, for the most part. Indeed, it made the decision on whether to rebuild Adamant Hall much simpler. The restoration continues apace, overseen by Dormid – who has recently progressed to a mighty wheeled chair from which he harries his minions.

And the process has received aid from a most unexpected source. His Majesty has visited us four times to make our dear hatchling's acquaintance (he has christened her Brighthelmstone, which I understand to be his pet name for his favourite seaside town – royalty are so whimsical, are they not!) and as he has the greatest dislike of draughts and damp, we have been descended on by the Ordinance Corps. The dear boys are a little bored since the end of the war – not to mention composite experts on making dilapidated chalets comfortable for officers and brigadiers at a moment's notice. Truly, who knew that a slate roof could be retiled in just two days with no fatalities whatsoever?

Oh, and a final thing. Both my brother's shade and that of the admiral have departed. Peregrine, I suppose, wished to impart news of the egg to his sister, but I wonder what mission the admiral managed to fulfil after all these decades? Was that ancient sea chest his? I suppose we will never know, but I am happy that he is at peace.

Alice James is a travel writer and photographer who also writes SFF and fantasy novels and short stories. Her series of romantic whodunnits, the Lavington Windsor Mysteries, is being published by independent publisher Solaris Press.

The Mirror Weir

Josie Jaffrey

Afterwards, they put barriers along the edges of the bridge, high enough that you could no longer see the water and what lay beneath it. But that was afterwards.

Before, there was only a waist-high railing separating the edge of the footbridge from a ten-foot drop to the rapids below. The locals called it the mirror weir, because the water is so clear where it runs over the edge that, from the bridge, you could see yourself reflected in the shadow of the structures beneath. Some people saw other things besides, or so the rumour goes, and it was a convincing rumour because it answered questions that were otherwise unanswerable. Why so many deaths, decade by decade, year after year? How could you explain the strange behaviour that preceded them? And why that spot specifically?

Nonbelievers would say it's not uncommon for drunken students to fall into rivers, and that people are willing to jump off practically anything when given the opportunity, whether they're seeking clout or oblivion.

But this story isn't for them.

Freshers' week. In a university city, revelry abounds. The new crowd heads to the centre, untethered, drawn by the siren call of drinks offers and bright flyers that beckon them to the loud and easy places, where their shoes will stick to the floor and their drinks will be served in test tubes, jam jars or glow-in-the-dark shot glasses, depending on the theme. But the old crowd, the graduate students and third-years, avoid those haunts. They seek out quiet corners to catch up with friends they've already made, and with whom they stuck to those same floors in years past. They're the ones, jeans-clad and unkempt, who walk over the bridge and down the towpath to the tree-filled beer garden of the Water Boatman.

It's a nice pub. A little dated, perhaps, but that's part of its appeal. It serves beer and ale, scampi fries and peanuts. The wine list is two bottles long, and the closest you'll get to a cocktail here is a gin and tonic. It's a magnet for real ale purists, and dog owners love the beer garden, but for everyone else it's just a pleasant place to sit and watch the river while they enjoy their pint.

Martin is not a casual customer. He has picked his venue carefully. He knows that Laura is an aficionado of ale, that she likes to walk along the towpath at the weekends, and that she stops to say hello to every dog she passes on her way. He's been thinking about her all summer – her ruthless grammatical precision in tutorials, the satisfied curve of her lips as she pieces together a translation, the way the library lights pick out the shimmer of red in her otherwise brown hair – and he's decided it's finally time to take the plunge.

"Fancy a drink at the Boatman?" he texted earlier this afternoon. Casual, no pressure, chill.

"Sure," came the response. "Six-ish?"

So here he sits in the beer garden as sunset approaches, one pint of ale standing ready for her across the table as he nurses his own – truth be told, he isn't a fan – and waits.

And waits.

There's a bug in Laura's glass. Martin fishes it out, then realises he probably shouldn't have put his fingers in her drink, but surely that's better than giving her a pint with a bug in it and she'll never know and they're clean, he's sure, at least they were before he covered them in ale. It's running down his wrist and he can't hug her with a wet hand – what would she think? – so he wipes it on his jeans but he can *see* it there like a stain, even in the twilight, and now she's going to think he's pissed himself or got really sweaty or something awful and oh god he shouldn't be this nervous about having a quiet drink with someone he's been friends with for two years.

Six o'clock turns into quarter past, turns into half past. Martin's jeans have dried and the sun has gone. It's a moonless night, so the only light left comes from a few solar-powered lamps that mark the path, and whatever pours out of the pub's front windows, both sources reflecting off the river in a kaleidoscopic scatter.

He hears her laugh before he sees her. At first it's welcome, a relief to know she hasn't stood him up for this date that she doesn't know is a date, but then he realises what it means: she's not alone. As she rounds the corner into the beer garden, they lock eyes and he tries to smile, despite the crowd around her: her two housemates, Serena and Ruth, along with three of the guys from their tutor group. James and Murad are okay, but Martin is less than happy to see RJ at Laura's shoulder, leaning in so close he must be able to smell her hair.

"Martin!" RJ yells. "Why are you sitting in the dark?"

He mumbles something about it being a warm night and watching the stars, despite the fact that there are none to be seen this close to the city, then he picks up his ale as the group ambles towards the pub's door.

"Is that for me?" Laura asks, smiling shyly at Martin as she gestures at the pint left sitting on the table.

"It was there when I got here," he says, abandoning all attempts at charm, because what's the bloody point?

Then, without looking back, Martin follows RJ inside.

Laura isn't sure how things got so out of hand. Everyone was excited to be back here for the new term, excited to see each other, and somehow they all got scooped up in Martin's invitation to the Water Boatman. The moment she arrived, she knew it was a mistake. He'd clearly been in the mood for a quiet drink with a friend, and she'd turned up with half their tutor group and turned it into something raucous. Why did she keep making these errors in judgement?

And RJ. *Ugh*. RJ.

So obnoxious. So brash. So handsy, as though their

misguided one-night stand at the summer ball gave him the right to fondle her forever. She should have pushed him off the bridge on the way over and been done with it.

"So," RJ says, flourishing a penny between his fingers. "Is everyone clear on the rules?"

They're sitting at a large round table in the middle of the pub, getting glares from the locals as they embark upon the third drinking game of the night. RJ has a bottomless repertoire, of course. The latest involves flicking a penny into a glass, then different people drink based on a complex system of nominations that no one except RJ seems to grasp. They all nod along nonetheless.

As with all the games this evening, somehow the rules require Martin to drink more and buy more than anyone else. Laura sees the vicious twinkle in RJ's eye and kicks him under the table. He takes this as a cue to put his hand on her thigh. She is in the process of extricating herself when Martin's head thumps down on the table top.

"Marty boy!" RJ crows. "You're wankered, my lad."

"And why do you think that is?" Laura asks, glaring at him as she finally eludes his grip. "You've been fucking with him all night. Why can't you just leave him alone?"

"He's a big boy, Laura. He can look after himself. He just can't hold his drink!"

James and RJ laugh, drunk and manic, but none of the others are smiling.

"Come on, Martin," Murad says, helping him out of his chair. "Let's get you home, mate."

"Yeah, it's late." Laura stands and shrugs on her coat. "I've had enough."

"Hey, come on now," says James. "Why are we breaking up the party?"

"Yeah, come on, Laura," RJ says, snaking an arm around her waist. "Have another drink."

"You know what, RJ?" Laura pushes him away, eyes blazing. "Fuck off. Fuck *all* the way off. And when you've finished fucking off, fuck off some more."

"Whoa," RJ says with a laugh, "calm down, love. Must be that time of the month. Am I right?" He sniggers and turns to James, who dutifully sniggers back.

Ruth glares at James. Serena calls RJ a sexist prick. Laura ignores them both and helps Murad get Martin back on his feet and out of the pub, with the other girls following behind.

When they reach the river, Laura is cuddled up between Serena and Martin. The towpath is wide enough for all five of them to walk abreast, clinging to each other for warmth and support.

"What the fuck was his problem tonight?" Serena slurs.

"RJ?" Laura murmurs back. "He's just being a dick."

"Because of what happened at the ball?"

Laura glances at Martin, but it's clear that he's not following their conversation, or any other conversation, for that matter. Instead, he's singing *Show Me the Way to Go Home* under his breath. Badly. He's cute when he's wasted, his mousy hair sticking out in all directions as his glasses teeter on the very end of his nose.

"I guess," she whispers to Serena. "I don't know why I let him come. This whole night was a fucking disaster. Poor Martin. He just wanted a quiet drink. I don't know how I'm going to make it up to him."

Serena smiles. "I think I have some ideas."

"Serena!" Laura fearfully glances at Martin again, but Ruth and Murad have joined in the song on his other side and the noise is easily muting their conversation. "What are you implying?" she continues, more softly. "Martin and I have been friends for years."

"And whose fault is that?"

"I don't know what you're talking about."

"Oh, come off it. You've fancied the pants off him since our first seminar."

"Will you keep your voice down?"

"Oh, relax. He's away with the fairies. Besides, would it really be the worst thing in the world if he found out how you felt? One of you is going to have to make a move sooner or later. I'd say it's your turn. You kind of ruined his go tonight."

Laura's feet stop moving. She only stays in motion because the others are pulling her along.

"You think he… Tonight?" she says after she's managed to pick up her feet and get them back in order.

"I'm pretty sure."

Laura sneaks another look at Martin and smiles to herself, then she and Serena join in the song, letting it carry them along the river, across the bridge and all the way home. The girls don't look down as they cross, so they don't see the shape beneath the water of the mirror weir.

But someone does.

Still, there's no sign that anything is wrong until the next morning.

Laura's hangover is possibly the worst of her life, and she's had enough of them that she's created her own hangover measuring system. Today, it's a ten point five: head in the toilet, kill me now, should have made herself sick last night because it would have felt better than this unending torture. Just as well that lectures don't start until next week, because there's no way she's dragging herself out of the bathroom this Friday morning. She can only imagine how Martin must feel.

They left the boys in the sitting room last night, Martin curled up on one sofa and Murad on the other. Martin seemed coherent enough after the bracing walk back, if a little distant, so Ruth gave them each a bucket, just in case, and left them to it. Truth be told, they were all too drunk to worry much about how drunk their friends were.

Until now. Laura expects to find Martin in exactly the same place when she eventually descends to the sitting room in her pyjamas, but although Murad is snoring happily, the second sofa is empty.

"Ruth?" she calls back upstairs. "Are you awake?"

"No," a groan replies. "Ruth is dead. There is no Ruth."

"And no Serena either," a second voice adds.

"Is Martin up there with you?" Laura calls.

"What? No!" Serena yells, at the same time Ruth says, "Who the fuck is Martin?" which Laura takes as a no.

She searches the house without finding any trace of him. She wakes Murad and asks if he knows anything, but he's been sleeping like the dead all night. She texts Martin repeatedly, then gets desperate and starts calling him instead. Still, there's no reply. Eventually, she throws on some clothes and starts walking towards his house. The route takes her over the river, over the footbridge to the other side of town.

It's an overcast day, so cloudy that it makes the morning dark. Perhaps that's why the shine catches her eye.

There's a pair of glasses in the water.

And, beyond them, a face.

Laura startles, expecting blank eyes and lifeless limbs, but that's not what she sees. Instead, his eyes twinkle through the clear water. His lips twitch into a smile. His fingers curl in invitation, as though he's simply standing behind a window, beckoning her inside, and she has the sensation in that moment that he *knows*. After two years of dancing around the truth, they can be honest about how they feel. The gulf between them has evaporated, not only because they now understand each other, but because he's so close. There's no drop to the weir, no water between them, nothing between their lips except a few inches of air that she could do away with if she just leaned forward and let them touch. He's only a breath away.

"Laura?" The voice draws her gaze from the water

and breaks the siren call. Serena is hurrying across the bridge towards her, a coat wrapped over her pyjamas. "What are you doing? It's freezing out here."

"Looking for Martin," Laura says, blinking away her dizziness. "I was going to go over to his place."

"I've called. He's not there."

"I saw–"

But when Laura looks back at the weir, there's nothing to see except the reflection of the two girls and the clouds above their heads. The water rushes ever onwards, down towards the lock.

That's where the police find his body, crushed in the mitre gates.

When RJ finally drags himself out of bed, he's filled with alcohol-induced regret. And real regret. God, he behaved like a prick last night. He's already thinking about calling Laura to apologise when James pushes into his room.

"Hey, how about knocking?" RJ yells. He likes to sleep in the nude, like a proper red-blooded man, but he is not cool with his housemates stealing a peek at his goods. Not the male ones, anyway.

"Have you seen the news?" James says, not slowing down enough to apologise.

"I just woke up. What do *you* think?"

"Martin's dead. They're saying he drowned."

RJ's first thought – *good riddance* – does him no credit, but even he recognises that it's a shitty response to finding out a sort-of friend is dead. Instead of saying it out loud, he asks, "Is Laura okay?"

"Not really."

It's an understatement. She refuses to talk to him over the weekend, despite many attempts to contact her via text, email, voicemail, letter and shouting outside her bedroom window. Ruth and Serena are giving him the cold shoulder too. Apparently it's his fault Martin got drunk and went wandering in the night, but it's not like RJ was buying the drinks, and it's not like it was RJ's sofa the idiot crashed on. RJ wasn't the one who left Martin unsupervised when he was completely off his face. Accordingly, he fails to see how the accident has anything to do with him. He'll say sorry anyway if it means Laura will talk to him again, but he can't get close enough to try. Monday comes, Tuesday and Wednesday pass, and still she doesn't turn up for classes.

Eventually, Serena sets him straight after Thursday's lectures.

"Leave her alone," she says through gritted teeth. "She doesn't want to talk to you."

"Why not? What did I do?" He deploys his hurt little puppy dog eyes. For the first time in his life, they don't work. To his surprise, Serena doesn't melt. Instead, her eyes fill with tears of rage.

"You were a fucking prick to him!" she yells. "All the time, every class, every time we hung out, every single moment. You couldn't leave him the fuck alone, and now you won't leave Laura alone either. If anyone's responsible for his suicide, it's you, and everyone knows it. So just fuck off and stop pretending you're the fucking victim, because it won't work."

Ruth takes Serena's arm and steers her away, leaving RJ alone on the pavement outside the lecture hall, trying to piece together his next move. To his mind, his predicament boils down to one problem: Laura thinks he pushed Martin to suicide. He simply needs to find a solution to that problem.

It's possible she's right; Martin always was a weak excuse for a man. He was just the kind of pathetic boy who'd take a joke the wrong way and end up getting everyone else in the shit when they'd done nothing wrong at all and really it was just that Martin was too fucking wet to act like a grown up.

But maybe she's wrong. Maybe Martin didn't commit suicide at all. And even if he did, maybe there's a way RJ can throw enough doubt on the question to get himself back into Laura's good graces. And, if all goes well, her knickers too.

RJ decides to dedicate himself fully to this project, so he starts skipping classes, too. Instead of attending lectures, he hangs out by the river taking photos and noting down everything he sees: the dimensions of the weir, the distance to the lock, the marks on the standings that hold the bridge steady. He sees Laura there sometimes, standing on the bridge and looking down at the weir for hours on end, as though she's hypnotised by the rushing water. He says hello the first couple of times, but that sends her scurrying back home without a word, so he learns to keep himself out of sight beneath the bridge. He can watch her from down here, following the lines of her face for as long as she follows the lines of the water. She never sees him, but seeing her is enough to motivate him to keep going.

His absences get worse over the coming weeks. Instead of learning advanced grammar and vocabulary in his seminars, he spends his days in his room trawling through the internet for articles about deaths in the area. This takes him to the library's microfiche room, where he scrolls through old newspapers and finds an eerie number of suspicious deaths connected with the mirror weir. For a C student who's barely cracked a book since the end of the summer term, he does good research. It almost gets him the real answer, the one he isn't even looking for, but the library is closing and he packs up his bag just one screen before he reaches the story that would explain it all. It's unassuming: three short paragraphs in an ancient paper.

Clairvoyant's Ill-fated Love Affair Prompts Triple Suicide

But RJ doesn't see this. Instead, he goes home and falls down a rabbit hole on the internet: college students are drowning all across America, all in mysterious circumstances, and all linked by graffiti of a smiley face found at the scene. He pulls out his photos of the bridge, sees what might be a scrappy smiley face spray-painted on the standings, and sets the hare running through conspiracies of murder cults and schools for assassins.

This will be his story.

Martin – gentle, inoffensive, wet-behind-the-ears Martin – was the target of an international syndicate of hitmen who've been operating around the world. Here's the proof: the smiley face, the fact he drowned, the similar disappearances in America, all signalling clearly that this criminal network has been established in the UK for decades.

RJ doesn't believe it for a second, but maybe Laura will, if he can present her with the right evidence. And if he can prove that Martin was a murder victim instead of a suicide, that'll be his job done, name cleared, pathway to Laura's pants once again unobstructed.

So he gets to work, locking himself in his room for days to prevent any distraction from the task at hand. In this, his prime objective, he is motivated. He prints out the relevant bits from the internet, running through all the ink in his housemate's colour printer to get the photos sharp. Then he goes back to the river with his expensive camera and gets up close to the smiley face graffiti, comparing his angles to the print outs so he can make his own crime scene photos resemble the ones on the internet as closely as possible.

He's concentrating so fiercely on his task that he doesn't see her fall. He didn't even realise she was here. He hears the splash, though, and turns in time to see something drop over the edge of the weir. It looked like a shoe.

At first, he thinks it's nothing. Probably a branch. But then he remembers the way Laura has been gazing into the water and he starts to wonder.

He runs down the towpath, eyes scanning the point where the weir crashes down into the river and beyond, searching for any sign of a shoe, a foot, a body. There's nothing.

Starting to doubt his own mind, he runs back the

way he came, cradling his camera in his hands, along the towpath and up the steps to the middle of the bridge, to the same spot where she has been standing, day after day.

He drops the camera to shatter on the ground at his feet. Taking the railing in his hands, he leans over to look down into the water, just as he has seen Laura do so many times before.

The weir is like a sheet of glass between them, cocooning her beneath its current as though she's surrounded by air, not water. It doesn't seem to move her at all. She looks like she's sleeping. Then her eyes open and fix on his. She lifts her hand beneath the water and waves. RJ would swear he sees triumph tilting the corners of her mouth, and he can feel her mocking him with her intention to go somewhere he can't follow.

He can't abide that. She can't drown. He hasn't won her yet. She's not *allowed* to drown. He won't let her leave.

So he jumps.

But RJ has been locked away in his room for days. He's out of touch. He doesn't know that Laura has been dead since last night, or that the police recovered her body from the lock this morning.

There's nothing in the weir but a soul waiting to be released; a role waiting to be filled.

In a university city, memories are short. Students move on, taking their stories with them, and people forget that more of them arrived at the beginning of term than left at its end. Twenty years on, the few locals who remember how many lives the mirror weir has taken are outnumbered by those who decry the way the new barriers block the view, or who argue that their height makes the bridge a hot spot for assault. It's not their fault. They mean well. They're not wrong, either, but they don't remember enough to balance the drawbacks against the danger they keep out.

In the end, they win.

The barriers are coming down next month. Beyond them, one soul has been waiting two decades for someone to replace him. He is unlikely to be kind to the one he takes.

Josie Jaffrey is an indie author of urban fantasy, paranormal romance and young adult fantasy who lives in Oxford, England. If you enjoyed this short story, you might enjoy May Day, the first book in Josie's Seekers series. It's an urban fantasy novel featuring a chaotic vampire detective with a serious grudge against the only man who can help her solve her latest case.

Netty and Eva

T. K. Howell

The voices in my head grew louder as the boat surged through the spray and Iona hoved into view. Aleister and Sir Arthur were right: something lingered. The war, Verdun, the Somme and everything that came after. It scrambled the brain. Aleister said he could feel it in there, if he looked hard enough: a trembling vibration in the soles of the feet, a flicker in the corner of the eye. There was something inside that wasn't me.

Netty heard the voices, too. I guess everyone in the Guild did. But she… Netty had always been… she got ideas into her head. And when she did, it was the devil's work to shift them. It made her do things like run to a tiny speck of an island on the edge of the Hebrides. And for what? Damned if I knew, but I felt duty-bound to find out. Since I'd given birth to Anna in '21, Netty and I were not the same. That link, that *pull* that existed between us, had slackened. Whether it was because I'd had a baby, because I was with a man, or because of who that man was, I don't know. Netty knew I wanted a child, and how else did she think I was going to do it?

It was cold, wet and windy. The sea chopped viciously the entirety of the short jaunt over from Mull. But after you'd seen Verdun through the eyes of a hundred walking dead men, it didn't really cut through. After you'd felt the non-stop barrage, each and every shell vibrating through your skull, a little light motion sickness didn't touch you. The hammering. It felt like a bass drum pounding underwater. It made me feel top heavy. It made me feel like my hindbrain was in control. Everything else was washed out. The voices came and went. They raked their nails down my spine. I shook my head and concentrated on the sound of the surf and the gulls and they eased off again.

There was a concrete slipway at the shore and I hopped out as the boat was tied safe. About thirty houses lined the bay, each made from slate-grey stone blocks the size of battleships. They matched the sky.

It wouldn't have taken five minutes of asking to find Netty. She always stood out, no matter where she was. But I didn't need to ask. I could still feel her itching at the back of my brain.

The voices came again. I ignored them and they died down, like always. Like the ringing in my ears that remained long after the bombardments. It wasn't even my ears that were ringing, but the ears of men long dead. I hadn't been within two hundred miles of any bombardment. The ringing was still there, though. It still persisted. Residual traces. For a decade, I'd learned to live with them. It was the fleeting glimpses that got to me. Boys in uniform with an arm blown clean off, suddenly shuffling into my peripheral vision, but disappearing when I turned my head. Did the rest of the Guild have the same? They never mentioned it if they did.

The Guild of Light. What a stupid, stupid name. Pompous, self-aggrandising, self-important. Sir Arthur all over. His loose collection of waifs, strays and underemployed aristocrats with too much time on their hands. People with the *gift*. Aleister, Sir Arthur, Frieda, Anand, Netty, Lars and the rest. And then me, the lost little girl Arthur picked up along the way. We played at it, at first. Parlour tricks, mostly. We dabbled and then the war came along and Sir Arthur was overtaken by a fervour to *do something*. So, by Governmental decree, we became the Ministry of Influence and Insight, England's first line of spiritual defence.

I found the guest house where she was staying easily enough. No trickery. No looking inside people's heads. No need. It took a while to beat that out of myself. I had always used the *gift* like a kid with a new toy, when there were simpler, more *polite* ways of getting what I wanted. Another lesson from my *social betters* at the Guild. Manners maketh the man. Or woman.

Netty'd had her own furniture shipped out, and that had made an impression on the locals. God only knew how much she was really worth. She never talked about it. Shipping up her own furniture for, what, a month? Two? I wish I'd known what she was up to. I read her scribbled note again, her handwriting an almost painful imitation of the one I'd known. All jagged. It looked like she had carved it into the paper.

A powerful case of healing. Must do this alone. Don't come.

But I still came. I never had a choice.

I reached the door of the guest house and was about to knock when I heard the clip-clop of solid, practical leather shoes on the cobbled, spindrift-strewn streets. I knew that gait, I could feel *her* marching down the street toward me. I could sense her anger like a yapping dog.

"Eva bloody Loveridge. What the hell are you doing here?"

"How's the baby?"

I had booked myself into the same guest house in a little room across the hall from Netty. We didn't let on that we knew each other. I didn't really know why. Habit, I guess. We were always so careful. One had to be.

Netty had grown gaunt and pale since I had last seen her four years earlier. Her eyes had become sunken and with the hook of her nose it gave her face the set of an irritated hawk.

"I said how's the baby?" There was a cold look in her eyes, a slight sneer.

"Anna. Her name is Anna and she's nearly eight years old. For God's sake Netty, how can you be jealous of a child? What's wrong with you? Are you ever going to stop sulking about it?" I said. She was tightly wound, I could feel it. Was it me? Was I making her anxious? Conflicting feelings bounced around inside her – love, pity, anger, shame. Her head, it was a mixed-up ball of colours, a thud and kaput of clanking scents, a cold, burning sound in the eyes.

And then there were the passengers. Thin, wispy

little things. Wraiths of cotton wool strand. The remnant of the syllable of a first name, the vague essence of a person. And terror... so much terror. They were there by the hundred, just the same as me. But I kept mine locked away. A hard clasped shell of a prison. Not Netty. Netty let them parade-ground march through the centre of her mind. Full kit and uniform, but all blown to hell, staring vacantly ahead.

"Stay out," Netty snapped. "We always said no looking without permission. You breaking your promise?"

"I just wanted to see you were… in order. You seem agitated."

"Of course I'm agitated."

"Good God, eight years, Netty. It was eight years ago. How else was I supposed to do it, eh?"

"But... did it have to be him? It ruined the group."

"You're exaggerating. Verdun broke the Guild. It broke us all. You think anyone gave a fig where Aleister put his–"

"Please, must you be so coarse?" Netty flinched.

"Frieda might wrinkle her nose, but she doesn't go around sticking it in other people's business. It's just you who over-reacted."

"I had a right to know."

I took a huge breath. "Look, that's not why I'm here. That's the past. Can't we just move beyond it? Netty, tell me what the hell you think you're doing up here. You know what this place is, don't you? Iona? It's a graveyard for the likes of us. It's where the druids used to come to die. And sometimes not willingly." I tried to wrap her up in a warm, loving embrace of pulsing reds and calming camphor. Netty glared at me with those predator eyes and I snapped it off straight away.

"None of that, Eva. Twice now. I won't warn you again." She arched her lip. "I'm here because I need to send them through. They're stuck, half *here*, half *there*. I need to heal them. This is the place to do it. I did some research, spoke to some people. They said it could be done."

"People? What people?"

"Never you mind."

"Netty, what people?" I asked forcefully. There was a tremor of something in my voice. Fear, I think.

Netty hesitated. "The German."

It was like a bomb going off in a bell foundry inside my head. There was a barrage like a pyroclastic flow that whipped through my brain for about three seconds. I had to sit down. After the noise died down, the voices came again. Subtle, insidious little voices, not speaking words so much as top notes of pain and suffering. Ghosts. Just ghosts. Memories of people. And then they were gone, pushed down and away.

"The *German*?" I tried to keep my voice level but it came out as a strained yelp. "What the hell were you thinking?"

"War's long over, Eva. We have to rebuild bridges, we have to work together. Can't ostracise them forever, you know. He was doing the same as we were. And they're his compatriots I'll be saving. We were all soldiers, really. Just as innocent as all those boys."

"Don't."

"We have to face it. Would you rather just live with those voices for the rest of your days?"

"Maybe we deserve to."

"What?" Netty frowned.

"I said maybe we deserve to. I've had Anna, Netty. And that means I've got somewhere to focus everything. I'm sorry that you stopped being most important person in my life. And I think… I think you got cut off from everything and that made you *like this*. That's my fault, I guess. But going it alone, it's no good for dealing with what we did. We went into the trenches. Maybe not physically, but we projected ourselves out there, into the minds under those helmets, and we tried to make them run, to shoot wide, to jam their guns. And when they died – when we killed them – a little bit of them got left behind. A trace. Maybe we deserve to live with that."

Netty looked down at her feet for a long time. She cocked her head to one side as if listening to distant voices, somewhere in a French field a decade gone.

"I can't," she said quietly. "I can't live with them and their pain any more. I need to send them through."

"At least let me get some of the others here. We might be able to do it together, but on your own..." I let it hang. Netty was strong, but I could feel all those voices bubbling and chuntering away at the front of her mind. I didn't need to be in her head to see it. She was living in a state of perpetual fear and disorientation. She was shell shocked.

"Tomorrow night, Eva. That's when I do it. It's the

time. I'm going to the mounds. I will open the door and send them through. Don't try to stop me."

"Do you remember what it used to be like?" Netty asked that evening. We were lying in front of an open fire, our legs tangled together, a blanket over us and a sheepskin rug underneath. It had happened quickly. We had gone up to our rooms alone after the landlady served us a plain dinner of potatoes and lamb stew. But we could feel each other moving around, each thinking about what the other was doing. I didn't even knock. I simply let myself in. We didn't speak, and for a moment, ten years just fell away.

"Well, *these* didn't use to droop quite so much," I said. "Be glad you've never breastfed, Netty. They'll suck the youth right out of you."

Netty frowned. It was a sore I shouldn't have picked at, even in jest. "I didn't mean *us*. That's not what I meant. I meant the Guild. The Ministry. When we were all working as one. Those nights sat in the hall at Athelney House, or out in the garden at dawn. Don't you remember how it felt when there were six, seven, eight, even twelve of us.? All linked, all thinking the same thing, the energy flowing between us in that great circle of will. I could feel it in every fibre of my being. I could feel *you*, I could feel all of us. It felt… it felt like it pulled at something deep from within my brain, something ancient. Atavistic, you know?"

"Hmm." I twisted my mouth and tried not to look her in the eye. "I remember mostly being terrified. Or, rather, projecting ourselves two hundred miles into the brains of Kraut soldiers who were terrified. After the first time, I could never really tell if the fear was theirs or mine. Both, I guess."

"Yes, but… but it was *something*, wasn't it? It felt like we had purpose. Don't you miss it? The energy? And then after, we would..."

"Hmm."

"Even after Verdun. Even after Anand–"

"Please, Netty."

"Even after Anand dropped dead. The blood from his nose. Good God. The blood. That's when I realised it wasn't just a game. It was *real*, it was *dangerous*. Not some abstract thing done at a distance. It was its own war. And after Anand it felt… better."

My eyes opened wide and I let out a long, low sigh. "Jesus, Netty."

"Every time it was like dancing the foxtrot all over a knife edge, staring Death in the face and daring him to make the first move. I've taken things, since. Things I got from a friend in Pharmaceuticals. It doesn't come close. And then we started to fall apart. Eight, then six, then five, until finally it was just the four of us and it was all over long before Armistice. Once we stopped, *they* all came crashing in on me. Hundreds of little German voices. Little slivers of each mind we dipped into, each one that died while we were connected to them." Netty tapped her temple forcefully with her forefinger, looked me in the eye and drew back her top lip. It was only a moment, but for that moment, she looked angry, close to tears. "When the work stopped, there was nothing to keep them quiet. To go from *that*, from what we did every day during the war, to *this*? A decade of nothingness. Me on my own, doing what I can. Little fleeting moments of what it used to be. Seances. My God, have you done seances, Eva?"

"Tell me you haven't," I frowned. "You can't–"

"Talk to the dead. Yes, yes. I know. Don't you think I know? I've done my fill of them, working with others who had as much *gift* as you do in your little finger. They're miserable. Such lies I tell. But you don't need to talk to the dead. You only need to read what's in the minds of those desperate to hear."

"Why? It's not as if you need the money."

"Haven't you been listening? To *feel* something like what we had again. To keep *them* quiet, for an hour or two."

"Is that what this is? A chance to relive past glories? On your own? You can't, Netty. You'll kill yourself."

"The German says it's possible."

I stood up abruptly and yanked the blanket away with me, leaving Netty lying naked and glistening in the fire-light. She didn't flinch or make to cover herself up. "The *German*. Good grief. And you believe him?"

"Maybe you should get back to your own room. Don't want the old bag downstairs to get the wrong idea. I know how you'd hate that." She put her hands behind her neck and glared at me. "Why did you even come here?"

"Your mind runs in strange channels Netty. I'm worried about you. Let me help. Tell me what the damn German said, I'll get a telegram to Aleister, we'll think of something."

"Can't wait, Eva. Can't wait a day longer. I'll do it on my own, like I have the last ten years."

"You're being a fool."

"Go home. Go be with your daughter. Forget about me. Again."

When morning came around, Netty found me waiting for her at breakfast with my arms folded and a stern look on my face. The landlady served us kippers and then porridge. We ate in near silence. As far as she knew, we could have been complete strangers.

"Forty-eight kings of Scotland were buried on this island," she said, doing her best to inform and educate. "Although, this was probably back in the days when you only had to own twenty sheep to be proclaimed a king. Druids, too. Lots of druids died here. Only, they didn't get a stone slab or an inscription in the church. They got–"

"Mounds," Netty answered. I raised my head, a spoonful of porridge halfway to my lips, and caught her eye.

"Aye. Place was thick with them. A last holdout. They say this place had special meaning for them. They say the fairy folk roam free." The landlady's eyes twinkled and she smiled a good-humoured smile. Netty looked down at her porridge.

"Fairy folk? Is that so?" I asked.

"Ho, yes. I can see you're a sensible God-fearing young woman, so I won't pull yer leg. Fairy folk! 'Course no one actually from the island would say anything so daft in all seriousness. That stuff's for the day trippers. But there's definitely something about the place, isn't there? Go walk the moors out there, the mounds are everywhere, lurking in the mist. Definitely something about the place. And I say that as someone who's lived here nigh on my whole life. You stand on one of the bigger mounds under a full moon and believe me, you'll start to wonder, too."

"It's a full moon tonight, isn't it?" I asked.

Netty stood up and wiped her mouth with her napkin. "If you'll excuse me," she said, and walked out of the kitchen and back to her room. The landlady waited until the sound of her footsteps died away.

"Strange creature, that one."

"How so?"

"Walks the island most nights. I've seen her through the window going out onto the moors. She'll catch her death. Talks to herself, too."

"She seems harmless," I said, knowing full well that she wasn't.

"Aye… aye, I'm sure she is. I do wonder what she's doing out there, though."

"Me too."

The voices came and went through the day. They were an irritation. Without Anna to fuss over, feed, get ready for school, wash, clean her clothes and on and on, I started to notice them more and more. I looked out of the window after breakfast and there was a young man lying on his back in the field behind the guest house. He sat in a crater of mud, the rim flickering with flame. Half his face was missing. I blinked and he was gone, but I could still hear him moaning. I wondered if it was the same for Netty. She was flighty, erratic, but I couldn't imagine what I was experiencing would drive her to such dangerous lengths. It must have been louder, incessant. When mine came, they were indistinct. I could never discern actual words or meaning. But that was the thing about our works. We went into the minds of all sorts, but German mainly. Emotions, feelings, instincts – they had a universal language. Oh, for the finer point stuff, like *Trench B will advance on the Northern Ridge at 2300 hrs*, you needed a smattering to get by. But to drive a platoon from the field in abject fear, we only ever needed the general essence.

Netty disappeared and didn't come back for supper. I told myself to leave her be, but I knew I wouldn't. I found her out on the moor as the sun began to set. The full moon was already out, hanging heavy over the horizon. She was sitting on the largest of the druid mounds. It was a low, sloping mound that rose gently to about eight feet. Around its base, sheep milled, oblivious to any ancient, mystical energy the place might or might not have. Their gentle bleating and the low mist clinging to the earth gave the whole tableau a grounded, pastoral feel. This was ruined by the sight of Netty, who was kneeling on top of the mound wrapped in a navy blue cape, frantically scooping earth away with her bare hands.

"What the hell are you doing?" I said, dodging sheep droppings as I stalked up the mound.

"Go away, Eva. You'll ruin it." Her dark hair was a spiky bird's nest on top of her head. Her cheeks glistened with sweat, despite the cold. Mud streaked her face and, I soon noticed, the rest of her body. Because beneath the cape, she was completely naked.

"Bloody hells, Netty. Have you lost your mind? You're going to freeze to death."

"Go away." She continued to dig at the soil, ignoring me. I looked down and noticed that she was in fact using a small knife to cut a cross-shaped piece of turf out of the mound.

"X marks the spot, is it? Come on, away from here." I reached down to grab her arm, but she turned on me. Her outstretched arm, muddied up to the elbow, pointed the knife upward at my face. Her eyes were wide and white, her yellow teeth bared. There was something feral about her, something I did not trust or dare to turn my back on.

"Look, over there." She swung her arm and pointed her knife to the south.

"You need to calm down." I twisted my head to follow Netty's knife, but saw nothing at first. Then, gradually, it crept forward through the sea spray and drizzle. A bank of coal-black mist. It slowly inched its way across the rocky outcrops of the island, not breaking its steady pace. It came on over the sheep fields, low but growing wider and wider.

"Oh Christ."

Finally, Netty stood up, leisurely stretching her legs out as though she had all the time in the world. She tried to keep her voice calm, but it wavered.

"Not another word, Eva. If you must stay, get off this mound and go and stand with the sheep."

"No."

"*Go*," she yelled and flicked her arm out, bringing the knife up at me in a slashing uppercut. I stepped back instinctively and almost lost my footing. I couldn't guess if the blade would have cut my face if I hadn't moved, but I wasn't taking any chances.

"Go. This needs blood, Eva. And I'm not averse to using yours." She made another loose, weak jab at me with the knife and this time I knew she didn't have it in her. So I stood my ground and waited. She narrowed her eyes at me, then kneeled again and continued digging.

Around us, the black fog rose. It stretched out as far as I could see, down to the bay, out across the water. I wondered how our landlady was taking it, but then I looked closer and waved my hands in front of my face. There was no fog. Not really. Only a fog inside my mind, only a fog for those with the right eyes to see it.

Soon, the sheep were little clouds floating in a black sea, and then they were gone as the fog crept up the sides of the mound, slowly but inexorably.

"Can you hear them?" Netty asked frantically. "Can you hear them?"

"No," I lied. In my head, the mutterings, the pained moans, the grumbles, were rising with the fog. "Stop this, Netty. This isn't what we do. We work in other's heads. We don't do 'spells'. This… this is different. I don't like it."

"Who said we had to like it?" Netty answered, but the fog was rising, rising, covering her little dirt cross, her feet, her knees, her mud-spattered legs. I watched as she lifted both arms in the air and looked up toward the sky. She said something indecipherable. Something in a tongue I didn't understand.

There were figures now. Things moving out there in the fog. Slumping, stumbling things. Moving in groups. I imagined I saw the iron spikes of pickelhaube helmets break the fog like seedlings pushing up through the black, black earth. There were masses of them. They came on, shuffling forward, as if that was all they knew how to do, as if it was the last order they were determined to follow even through death.

Netty stared out at them with her feral eyes. They were gone, those eyes. Finally gone. I saw them and knew that Netty would not be back. I knew now that Netty had been gone ten years. The girl I had known since Verdun had only ever been a shadow. She turned the knife in her right hand, gripped it in a fist and brought it down hard on the palm of her left hand. But I never saw it hit. The fog swallowed it. All I saw was her face and her eyes. They didn't flinch or waver, even as I heard the hard thud of the impact. It must have punched the blade clean through her hand, but she didn't utter a sound. And then the face too was gone. There was the soft, crumpling sound of a body falling forwards, the voices in my head reached a crescendo and then they and the fog were simply gone.

A deep, black night fell as I sat on the mound next to Netty's body. The full moon seemed to cast a single spotlight on her alone. It didn't touch the inky void of the moors below. If I stepped off the mound would I simply fall away? Would I go wherever the voices went? I stroked her hair, but she was already turning cold. Her open eyes stared glassily out at the nothingness. I didn't close them. I made no effort to cover her naked body with her cape. What good would that do? But I waited with her. I waited, teeth chattering, fingers turning numb, until the first rays of light lanced across the moor and washed the void away.

I boarded the first boat off Iona that morning, making a brief stop to make sure our landlady forgot all about me. I tore out the sheet from the guest book where I had signed my name and I burned Netty's journal.

The crossing was calm. The only sound I heard was the light crashing of waves and the screech of the seagulls, which followed me all the way back to the mainland.

T. K. Howell is a writer living on the banks of the Thames. When not writing, he manages ancient oak woodlands and tends to trees that are older than most countries.

The Last New Bloods

Laura Jayne McLoughlin

Since Luthais was old enough to hold a sword, he knew that he wanted to be part of the Stone Hands of the West.

Though his village was ninety miles from the Frontier, he often heard of the Stone Hands' great exploits in advancing the country's territory. There were many guilds positioned along the Frontier – that long mountainous belt between the lands of chaos and those which had been civilised by the emperor – but it was the Stone Hands who ate up miles on the maps fastest. They were an elite crew of warriors who had claimed twice the mileage of any other Frontier guild in the last five years and had become exceedingly wealthy because of it. Merchants grappled for deals with them for trade routes; lords and ladies donated great sums to plant their flags on the claimed earth.

Supposedly, they had started out like any other guild, as a small collection of scrappy fortune-seekers, but everything had changed when Tormod the Vast took the helm.

He was said to be as vast as the mountain range the guild built their homestead upon and just as inhospitable, but he was a genius with an axe and no monster could best him. It was he who first rid the Wells of Delvy of the vampires which had long controlled them, and he who won the Killinglam Mountains for the kingdom from the trolls who had called it their home – the list went on, but what mattered the most was the coin the emperor awarded guilds for advancing the front line.

When Luthais was growing up, he and the other boys played at being monster hunters. All of them wanted to be Tormod, but it was only ever Aonghus who got to claim that title.

Aonghus was Luthais's best friend. He was the best fighter in their small group, no matter which weapon was handed to him, and his father had been a member of a lesser guild in his youth – one of the very few men who had actually returned from the Frontier.

"Dad said to swing it that way," Aonghus would tell Luthais. "You do it the way you are, and even the bears will kill you."

It was no surprise, therefore, to Luthais or any of the others that as soon as Aonghus turned seventeen, he set off for the Killinglam Mountains to join the Stone Hands during their recruitment ceremony – and it was for a mere six months' difference in their birthdays that Luthais did not go alongside him.

"I'll show you around when you get there," were Aonghus's last words to Luthais as he saddled his family's mare for the journey. His lisp caught on the *S*s and it was the only sign to Luthais that his friend was nervous. "Just don't embarrass me."

They laughed and Luthais gave him a good-natured punch on the arm.

"See you next year," Luthais said, and he meant it with his whole heart.

Two months later, when winter was beginning to take hold in the lowlands, Luthais received word of Aonghus's death. It was to be expected that at least ten or twelve boys would die each year when the Stone Hands took on new recruits – monster attacks, training accidents, the mountain itself – but Luthais had never considered that one of them would have been Aonghus.

Luthais cried longer and harder than he ever thought possible, and all winter, he waited. He waited with bated breath for his turn to come so that he might go to the Stone Hands and win. He waited to win for them both.

Against his mother's wishes and the requests of his village, Luthais arrived at the top of the Killinglam Mountain with a tattered rucksack and a hunger like he had never known.

He was greeted with handshakes and slaps on the back by some of the largest men he had ever seen. Each warrior he half-guessed was Tormod the Vast, but he was corrected time and time again. The other recruits gathered about the courtyard, appearing equally tired and battle beaten. There were more than he thought there would be – by the stories, most years only saw around fifteen new sign-ups, but this looked more like double that.

But he knew there were more still who hadn't made it. That was the first test of the Stone Hands: climb the mountain by blood and by sweat and reach its summit by the summer equinox, or die trying. Even to die on the mountain was preferable to returning home empty handed, knowing fully that you were the coward you always feared you would be.

They waited some time more, and a few other young men joined the group. Soon, the warriors began a chant, and Luthais knew this was all of them – twenty-six recruits, by his count.

"New blood," the Stone Hands chanted. "New blood running."

To this grim song, they were led inside the homestead. Snow had blown through the opening, coating lush furniture in a fine dusting of white, but as they pushed further into the mountain, the walls became craggy and dry, and the true wealth of the Stone Hands became apparent.

The main atrium was more luxurious than any room Luthais had ever laid eyes on. Where his home village hall might see some shine and glitter come Solstice celebrations, it could not compare to the exoticism and abundance showcased by the Stone Hands. Plush rugs of red and purple coated the floor. Fine tapestries in foreign languages dressed the walls, and hung across every chair and bench in the room were furs and skins from the Stone Hand's victories, from the grey pelt of a common wolf to ragged scaled hides Luthais couldn't place.

Overhead was a chandelier of many candles, which

lit the cavern with a warm glow, and standing directly beneath it was a tall, thin man in grey robes with a wolf pelt worn as a hood.

"My name is Tormod the Vast," he declared. "You have been welcomed to the homestead of the Stone Hands of the West. You may, too, someday call it home, but today, you will call it the Fire, for within it you will either be forged as great warriors to serve the guild and the advance of the Frontier line – or be burnt up as kindling. Are you ready to begin?"

The new recruits roared their agreement, Luthais among them.

As it had always been since last winter, he wanted to turn to Aonghus – to see his expression, ask his opinion, see what he thought of this "vast" Tormod they had fantasised about since boyhood – but there was no one there.

That night, sleep was hard to come by. There was the anticipation, the chill, then the sound of a dozen strange and unfamiliar snores in the room, and most unsettling, the feeling that there was someone watching him in the dark. More than once, Luthais sat up, expecting a pair of dark eyes blinking at him from a cot across the room, but all he found was two dozen sleeping boys.

All too soon, the new bloods' wardens arrived at the dormitories, and before the sun had risen, twenty-six young men were led out onto the mountain's craggy bluffs. They walked perhaps five miles over rock and through snow until they came to an abandoned outpost, which they were instructed to clear of wolves.

Wolves were a common predator at home and Luthais had killed more than his fair share protecting his village's livestock; the other new bloods must have had similar experiences, for there was soft laughter and noises of confusion amongst them.

All amusement dried up, however, once the wardens left them and the recruits saw their opponents. Rather than sleek grey creatures, these wolves were monstrous things of stiff black fur; there must have been something of witchcraft in how quietly their weighty paws fell upon the snow.

Then came the cloud. It was low-lying and thick, and it rendered the already unfamiliar land completely unknowable. The boys were blind and soon the only tell that someone had been picked off was a short, sharp scream before terrifying silence.

The guild members did not return for the new bloods until midnight. By then the wolves were gone and there were fifteen boys left.

Luthais survived, but it unsettled him to know how easily and quickly he might not have.

He passed the broken body of a boy whose name he scarcely knew and thought that if he had simply stayed at home, he might have been his town or city's best defender, their noblest knight. Today, though, on the icy peaks of Killinglam, he was but a failed recruit of the Stone Hands of the West.

He reached for the body, removing a blanket from his pack to wrap it with. The other boys did the same, but the wardens instructed them to stop.

"Leave them," the guild members ordered. "We

don't take the bodies."

Instead, the wardens cast handfuls of unknown grey dust about them, and where the dust landed, there was a soft hissing as if it burned, though the snow looked untouched.

"Now we go."

Luthais looked from the grey body in the snow to the grave expressions of his wardens. He folded his blanket back into his pack with reluctance, and without another word, fifteen boys and their wardens left for home.

The bodies stayed and the snow buried them instead.

Upon the seventh day, the guild celebrated the new bloods' victories. Mourning the losses was discouraged.

The new bloods were given the responsibility of rolling the barrels of drink from the lower floors to the atrium, which left Luthais and the rest panting for breath. It was a dog's job, really – one of many to come for the Stone Hands' new bloods, Luthais imagined.

It was a night of roaring and singing, drinking and dancing, and when a hired troop of dancers from the Southern marshlands entered the main atrium, the air turned electric with excitement and lust.

Luthais tried to carry on with the frivolities, but it felt mismatched to the week he had endured. His muscles burned, his joints ached, there was a lump on the side of his head from a ricocheting arrow he was lucky had not pierced his temple, and he could not help but feel the absence of his fellow new bloods like a physical weight on his back.

Maybe if it had not been for Aonghus, he could have cast aside the weight of these losses. They were a group of just ten now, which felt utterly unsustainable for the rest of these five weeks, but the other warriors assured them this was normal. The first losses were the quickest, and the last weeks were about picking off the stronger recruits in search of the strong*est*.

Luthais, despite surviving this long, did not feel *stronger*. He just felt lucky, and undeservedly so, and he left the atrium for the solace of the empty dormitories.

In the dark, Luthais was still unable to shake that watched feeling he had had since his first night here; he was beginning to think it would never leave. Perhaps he would always feel *watched*, and uncomfortable, and too sensitive, and perhaps he would always cry when they left bodies out on the mountain.

He was eighteen now. He didn't think it was meant to feel like this.

"Luthais?"

A voice bloomed from the darkness. For a moment, Luthais thought it was a dream, and that he was more tired than he had realised, but then he sat up, and the stone wall beside him was cold and rough, and the sheets beneath him balled so realistically, he could not think of anything else but waking life.

And yet Aonghus, who no longer belonged to waking life, was here.

Across the way, he sat with his elbows on his knees

on another recruit's bed. Luthais would have known his sloping smile and untidy head of hair anywhere.

"Aonghus," Luthais answered. "Aonghus, are you…"

He was on his feet then, rushing to his friend. He wanted to feel the heat of his body, the touch of his skin. He wanted his entire body to be pressed against Aonghus's and to know that he was here, solid and heavy with living.

And then, he reached him, and his outstretched hand, going for the shoulder, passed right through him.

Luthais ripped his hand back, cradling it as though he had stuck it in the fire, and he looked at his friend – really looked. Was there evil in his eyes? Was this a shapeshifter demon from the wilds, sneaking into the homestead while the warriors were otherwise occupied? By all Luthais could see and hear, this *was* Aonghus – light-haired and sweet, tall and a little gangly, but one could never be too careful in the mountains.

"Is that you, Aonghus?" he said.

Aonghus looked vaguely embarrassed and then answered, "I'm sorry I scared you."

It was the most Aonghus-like thing that he could have said, and with the catch of the lisp, Luthais almost tried to hug him all over again.

Gathering himself, he thought it better to sit beside him instead.

"I've been here a while," Aonghus said. "But I didn't know how to talk to you."

"You can always talk to me."

Aonghus shook his head. "You know what I mean.

It's not that simple, is it? Not when I'm… And you're…"

He seemed lost for words, but Luthais needed to hear them. He needed it said out loud.

"You're dead, Aonghus."

"I am, Luthais."

They sat in silence for a minute. Maybe more. It could have been an hour for the way Luthais's hands trembled and heart sped.

"It was last year," Aonghus said at last. "During training."

"I know. They sent your family a letter."

"What else did they tell you?"

"That was it. We couldn't even burn your body on the pyre because–"

"No, what did they say? How did I die?"

"Just… during training. How… How did you die, Aonghus?"

"I was murdered."

The words were cold and distant. They felt too grave to be true.

"Murdered?" Luthais repeated. "Someone *killed* you?"

"Yes," Aonghus said. "And someone will kill you, too, if you don't get out of here."

Luthais wracked his brain for understanding. "You died during training, Aonghus. The Stone Hands told us in their letter. Why would they lie?"

"Why do you think?" Aonghus asked. "They're the ones who murdered me."

Despite going to bed hours before the other new bloods even left the party, Luthais got just as little sleep, if not less. Aonghus's words were an ever-tightening noose and his very appearance a sudden hole in the ground.

He walked through the next day's trial in a daze. It was a wonder he didn't fall victim to the monster at hand: a large stag-like beast with scales instead of fur and a web of snakes for antlers.

The other new bloods told him as much, too, slapping him around the back of the head on their way home.

"Milksop," they called him. "Milksop the Gentle."

But he did not feel gentle. He felt violent with the knowledge in his head – so much so that he almost wished Aonghus had not appeared to him at all.

The Stone Hands of the West were murderers. That was the single point around which Luthais felt himself spiral. And if Aonghus – if it *was* Aonghus and not a monster in his skin or a hallucination – was to be believed, they were not common, rash killers, so used to bloodshed that they might simply shed a little more, but organised and precise.

"I have been here the entire year since I died, waiting so that I might warn you before you come to the same fate, and I watched more boys than just myself be murdered. They don't put you out on those hills to see how well you can fight, Luthais. They do it because they know at least some of you – of *us* – will fail."

Luthais had tried to argue with him – that the Stone Hands were the best and so expected the best, that training was supposed to be difficult, that they signed up to this knowing that the wheat would be separated brutally from the chaff – but Aonghus had more answers than Luthais could rebuff.

“You know as well as I do that something is wrong with this place. You’ve felt it since you arrived. They never take the bodies home. They sprinkle them with salts instead. And Tormod the Vast? I could have killed him myself, never mind the monsters of the Frontier. It is not right, not right at all.”

“And what does it mean, if it is not right? I have come to be a warrior.”

“But you may die a sacrifice.”

“A sacrifice? For what? To whom?”

“The Frontier’s beasts. There is a spell or a curse or *something* at work, for in the last year, over two dozen boys have died, and everyone is cast with the same light dust, and after that – Luthais, you wouldn’t believe it, but after that, the monsters out in the wilds? They just leave. They turn away and they don’t bother the guild at all. I am sure it is by these deaths they have gained the ground they have, how they have made their riches.”

Luthais had shaken his head. “The Stone Hands are good. We know they are good. They…”

And Luthais hadn’t known what to say then, because he didn’t have any more answers. He didn’t know why they couldn’t bring bodies home. He didn’t know why they had left a dozen boys out in the freezing cold for animals to devour, and he didn’t know why the only honour they showed them was a scattering of grey salt.

And yet it was madness to think that the Stone

Hands – a hardy band of leather and steel warriors – had anything to do with dark magic. He didn't think there was a single wizard in the entire guild, nor had he seen any sorcery books or diagrams. He hadn't even overheard a conversation referencing anything more magical than using nut oil to help seal wounds more quickly.

"See," Aonghus had said then. "You are upset, because you know that I am right, and it frightens you."

"I'm upset because you are here at all!" Luthais had cried, suddenly tearful. "I am upset because I want you to be here in body instead of just spirit, and I want us to go through this trial together and win like we always said we would, but we can't, because you are – You're dead, Aonghus, and nothing in my life has ever been as good as when you were here."

Aonghus had shaken his head like he had forgotten what it was like to run hot with emotion. Leaning close, he said, "I do not expect you to believe me or act this night, but I have waited a long time in this dreadful place because I knew I would meet you here and I want you to live."

"But I am frightened, Aonghus. How can I know I haven't dreamed you up entirely?"

"In Tormod's chambers," said the ghost, "you will find a portrait of a black wolf. Its eyes are blood red and there is a scar that runs along the left eye. There is nothing magical or enchanted about it, but it is there and if I know this much, then you can be assured that I also know how I died – how I was a sacrifice to this guild's greed."

Their conversation had ended abruptly when a new blood staggered into the room and vomited in the middle of the floor. Luthais had jumped to help him, but the boy simply waved him off and went on his way, and by the time Luthais looked back to the bed upon which he had been sitting with his best friend, it was empty.

There was only evidence of one person having sat there.

A total of ten days went by before they lost another recruit.

It felt fresh and unfair after so long without a loss, especially because the trials they were facing felt rather safe compared to those first days, when they had been instructed to go head-to-head with monsters. Now, if they saw a wolf or a scaled deer or anything similar, it was shot with an arrow before it might attack.

There had even been a day when a wolf had strayed right in front of their path while out on mission, and it had been so grisly and skinny that Luthais knew there was no other way out of this than to kill it. Hungry creatures were desperate ones, and desperation was dangerous. All the boys had steeled themselves for the attack, but it never came. After looking at them for maybe thirty seconds, the wolf turned its lamp-like eyes away, loped behind a few boulders and out of sight.

Luthais had been sure it was merely coming around from the back, to attack from a better angle, but it never returned, and that night, he lay awake thinking once again – always and forever – of Aonghus's words.

They don't bother the guild at all.

Though the monsters of the Frontier had become increasingly sparse, the mountain itself was not so meek.

It was a routine journey from one of the eastern peaks to collect the eggs of a rare eagle to be presented to a well-paying merchant, and one Luthais had been happy to be part of, but then bad weather rolled in.

It was like that first mission all over again when the cloud covered them, but worse entirely, because this time there was wind and snow to contend with, both of which drove the new bloods off course. The monsters of the Frontier appeared to have lost their bite, but the same could not be said of the mountainside or the cold.

By morning, the snowstorm had passed, but there were only nine boys left.

The body had fallen by a small turquoise plant.

"Ice-forged rose," one of the boys identified, and the group drew back.

It was a simple thing – four petals, bell-like flowers – but it stood out against the snow like a beacon in the dark. It was a deadly thing, spitting venom without warning, and the tell-tale signs of its poison were in the pocks across the fallen boy's face.

"Come on, Milksop," they called to Luthais when he hung back on the peak. "What are you waiting for?"

Luthais felt his feet rooted to that spot in the snow. He didn't know how to go home as part of a group of nine rather than ten.

"We should bring him home," he told the group, and they shook their heads.

"We're not supposed to bring anyone home,

Milksop. They stay on the mountain."

But Luthais didn't like that, and the other boys left without him.

Luthais knew that there would be trouble waiting for him back at the Stone Hands' homestead. He just didn't realise it would be with someone worse than one of the new blood wardens, and when he was instructed to visit Tormod's quarters immediately, something like regret flared in his gut.

Tormod's quarters were deep in the homestead, protected by two other warriors who stood guard outside his door. They permitted Luthais to enter, knowing smirks on their faces.

Upon entering, Luthais was surprised. Somehow, he had assumed Tormod lived in a cave of a place, all axes and swords hanging on the walls, suits of armour lining the space. Instead, the room before him was tidy. It had a desk and many papers, a wall of books and some spoils of war: pelts, helmets, a bone-white skull with a crack zigzagging from the left eye.

Tormod's hands were steepled beneath his chin.

"I hear you disobeyed an order today," he said.

"Yes," Luthais answered. "I did, but only because I believed that the order was wrong."

"And what do you believe now?"

Luthais took a breath. "That I should not have disobeyed my warden."

"Do you know what keeps a guild like this one alive?" Tormod asked, rising from his chair. "It's cohesion, new blood. Do you know what that means? It means to work *with* one another rather than against. When new bloods come here, we train them in the way that we do so that they are either a functioning and useful part of its body – or discarded as a cancer."

Luthais nodded.

"And while returning a friend's body is often a sign of respect and honour, here it is nothing more than a disgrace to that cohesion. You were told to leave the body. You let your brothers go on without you and you may have cost them their lives in doing so."

"I'm… I'm sorry for my ignorance. I only thought–"

"It does not sound like you are sorry enough."

Luthais looked up to see Tormod holding a leather strap. The old grey man gestured for Luthais to hold his hand before him, and with reluctance, Luthais did.

The strap came down on Luthais's palm a total of twenty-six times – one for every recruit who had arrived at the Stone Hands' homestead on that very first day. At first, it stung, then it burned, and when it seemed as though the pain would be unbearable, there was just a terrible numbness and blood spattered on his sleeves.

When Tormod was done, he cleaned the strap with his bare hand and cast the blood onto the floor.

"Being part of my guild requires sacrifice, new blood. Do you understand that?"

Luthais looked up. He blinked. "Yes, sir."

"Now get out of my sight."

Luthais turned to leave the same way he came in and came to a sudden stop. Above Tormod's door hung a small dark portrait. Two ears, a set of yellow teeth and one scarred blood-red eye marked it as familiar, and Luthais's blood, which still pounded in his hand, was suddenly cold.

"I said, *get out*," Tormod barked.

"I'm sorry," Luthais said, not quite turning – not yet. "I only– My friend saw a picture like this once, a long time ago. It is quite different. Unique."

Tormod settled behind his desk.

"His name was Aonghus," Luthais continued. "And he died during training last year. Did you know him?"

Only when Luthais looked back at him did Tormod answer. His expression was unconcerned.

"No. I don't keep count of the pups."

Luthais nodded. "I thought not," he said, and took his leave.

The party that evening was the last of the Stone Hands of the West.

Again, barrels of ale and wine were ordered to be rolled into the atrium, but Luthais told his brothers to go on. Tormod the Vast himself had told them to go out to the mountainside to keep watch, and as punishment for his disobedience, Luthais was to roll every barrel upstairs by himself. The new bloods found it a harsh punishment, but not undeserved, and they traipsed outside with their packs and short swords.

When he was alone, Luthais set to work.

It was clear to him that Tormod was right. The guild was one body, its members knotted by purpose and intention – by sin and sorcery. It was not enough to leave the guild, nor to get rid of Tormod himself, for Tormod's ways were not a part of him alone. No, he had infected the rest: each warden who carried out his orders, each warrior who pushed further into the Frontier.

The poison was easy to come by. There were rows of deadly items just waiting to be picked over in the guild's cellars and stores, but Luthais preferred the bright, mild-flavoured pollen of an ice-forged rose.

When the barrels were in place, he left to stand watch with the other new bloods. They laughed and joked and talked into the night, shivering against the relentless winter cold, and they thanked their Milksop for trying to move that body, because they truly hated rolling those barrels upstairs.

When the music stopped, they began to suspect something was wrong, but Luthais convinced them to stay out a little longer. By morning, though, they could not be persuaded, and he followed them inside the atrium, where a mass of bodies was slumped on the floor, across chairs, on top of each other. It looked, somewhat, like they had succumbed to a drunken stupor, their goblets lying nearby and splashes of ale upon their clothing, but their faces were too grey and their eyes too glassy.

The new bloods panicked, pulling at their fallen wardens with desperation. Luthais did not leave immediately, though he might have. Instead, he went in search of Tormod the Vast, and there he found him, cold hand still gripping a goblet, staring straight ahead.

He looked anything but vast in that moment, and

Luthais thought of all the little boys in villages who would cry on the day they heard someone had murdered their great and powerful Tormod, champion of the Frontier.

He thought, too, of all the little boys who would fight another day because Tormod was no longer.

Out on the mountain, a lone figure left the homestead, tracking a deep trail through the snow. He did not go in the direction of the villages, but along the line of the Frontier.

There were other guilds, Luthais reasoned, guilds which did not need to know where he had come from or what he had done. Guilds where he might do good. Guilds which were kind and honourable at their heart, which raised up their youngest instead of throwing them to the fire.

And if not?

Luthais knew how to handle them, too.

Laura Jayne McLoughlin holds a BA (Hons) in English with Creative Writing from Queen's University, currently works as a Digital PR Executive and writes short stories like this one in her spare time.

Unfinished Business

Adie Hart

The shop looked normal from the outside, but that didn't mean anything. Cedric had handled plenty of hauntings, albeit from the administration side of things, and not all of them took place in the kind of decrepit, cobwebbed old manors you'd expect. People tended to stick to what they knew, after all, and ghosts were just people.

Well. Ex-people.

Cedric squinted at the front of the building again. It was a nice shop, in a decent part of town; the building was old, but well-kept and brightly white-washed. A large bay window presented a dazzling array of bottles and boxes in a multitude of shapes and colours. A cheery purple sign proclaimed "Hawthorne and Daughters" in flowing letters overhead, and the wooden door stood invitingly ajar.

It certainly looked like a regular alchemist's shop, but Cedric's casebook confirmed this was the right place. Fourteen complaints from the neighbourhood about ghostly activity, from your bog-standard nighttime wailing and spooked cats to the more sinister physical effects, which indicated this ghost was both strong and dangerous. Books flapped their pages; candles guttered; furniture upended itself. One woman had reported that she'd come downstairs in the morning to find all her stockings had been arranged on the kitchen table to spell a rude word. Cedric prodded the page in the hope that the book would elaborate on that one, but though the letters swirled and reformed, it was only to clarify: a *very* rude word.

He snorted. Trust the investigation team to have equipment as humourless as they were. He tucked the casebook away and checked his belt one last time; the wand, potion case, and knife felt awkward against his hip, a weight he hadn't felt since graduating some fifteen years before. For what felt like the hundredth time, he cursed whichever idiot had brought the pixiepox to the Guild and laid out half the field wizards; to add a bit of variety he cursed Archwizard Tarquin too, for insisting the administrative team took up the slack. Cedric hated fieldwork. Desks didn't bite.

But even his most inventive curses didn't alter the fact that he was here now, and there was a ghost that needed exorcising. Cedric sighed, and stepped into the shop.

The cheery jangle of the bell made him jump, and he scolded himself under his breath; no one was going to take him seriously if he acted like a nervous rabbit. Tutting, he looked around to assess the situation, trying to see it as an investigator might.

Well. There was definitely something very wrong here.

The exterior of the building had indicated a fairly upscale business; he supposed the room was large and airy, but it was filled with such chaos that it genuinely took his mind a moment to register "shop". Like most alchemist's shops Cedric had visited, the front of the room was dotted with small tables and racks for product displays; along the back was a generous tiled workspace that resembled the offspring of a kitchen and a laboratory, and a door that presumably led to a storeroom. Unlike any other alchemist's shop Cedric had visited, not a single flat surface was visible. And very few vertical ones, now that he thought about it.

On the marble work table, a stack of beribboned boxes teetered precariously above a morass of alchemical paraphernalia even he would struggle to name. Tools lay scattered like fallen leaves; bottles twinkled like gems from baskets balanced three-high. In the sink, enough cauldrons to outfit an entire graduating class of wizards trickled tinted liquid over broken vials and crumb-covered plates. One wall was almost totally obscured by crates in a haphazard tower, and everywhere he looked there were scraps of paper covered in violent scrawls. The place was a disaster. If he hadn't known better, he could easily have believed he'd been sent here to clear out a flinderbat hoard; as it was, this was clearly the work of a very destructive ghost.

Cedric bent to pick up a stool that had been knocked over, but as he set it upright his cloak tangled around a narrow-legged table and sent a cascade of small tins clattering to the ground. Muttering to himself, he bent down once more.

There was a tremendous crash from the storeroom. The door rattled in its frame.

Cedric drew his wand and, longing for his desk, steeled himself for an attack. "If there is a presence here, announce yourself!" he cried.

And then the door burst open.

A figure staggered out into the room, and it took Cedric a moment to realise that rather than some shambling, flapping, square-framed monster with its legs on back-to-front, it was in fact a petite woman in an apron, walking backwards and dragging a large crate.

Somewhat sheepishly, Cedric tucked his wand back into his belt and watched the woman forge a path to the worktable through the piles. Twice she knocked into a display rack, and would have sent it flying if he hadn't darted behind her to steady it. When she finally reached the worktable, she gave an enormous sigh, shoved a basket onto the floor, and started unpacking jars into the newly-vacated space.

She still hadn't noticed him. Cedric began to see how the ghost situation could have got so bad, with a hauntee this oblivious. He cleared his throat.

The woman screamed and swept up a pan from the bench, rounding on him. Cedric threw his hands up, backing away. "Sorry, sorry!"

"Oh, a customer! Good morning," she said with a little laugh, setting down the pan on top of something that made a distressing *crunch*. "Sorry, I was a bit distracted and you startled me. Give me a few minutes?

I'll be with you as soon as I've got this potion on the boil." Without waiting for his answer, she started rummaging in the crate again.

"It's afternoon," Cedric said, then mentally kicked himself. That hadn't been what he'd meant to say at all.

"Oh, stars, is it?" There was a groan in her voice that spoke of total exhaustion. "The day's going far too fast. Okay, sorry, I'm all ears." She straightened and wiped her hands on her apron, suddenly looking much more like a shopkeeper. "What can I do for you? If it's for the festival, I'm all out of luck tea and hangover jam, but I'm just about to whip up a fresh batch of patter potion if you're looking to charm that special someone tomorrow." A cheeky smile lit up her freckled face, and Cedric's heart stuttered. That was odd. It must have been the adrenaline.

"No, I'm not– I don't need– look, I'm not a customer. I'm here about the ghost."

Cedric wasn't sure what kind of reaction he'd been expecting from the woman on hearing the word "ghost" – sometimes people were relieved, sometimes they were terrified – but he really, really hadn't been expecting her to roll her eyes.

"Oh, for the love of–" Abigail sighed, rubbing a hand across her brow. This was the last thing she needed, today of all days. She was already so behind on festival orders, and there were still Mr Stewart's regular tisanes to make after that, and there were gifts to buy for her nieces, and she didn't know *when* she was going to be able to fix that hole in her red dress before the feast…

and the wizard was still waiting for her response. She gave him her best customer service smile. "I'm sorry, I think you've had a wasted trip. There's no ghost here. Thank you for checking up on me, but as you can see, I need to get on."

The wizard looked confused. "This is Hawthorne and Daughters Alchemy?" When she nodded, he continued, "The Guild has had several complaints from your neighbours about ghostly disturbances. I was told that operatives visited last month to secure the premises, but clearly more power was needed to truly remove the spirit."

"And you're more power, are you?" Abigail said archly. He didn't look much older than her, perhaps thirty-five at most? Still, it wasn't a good idea to annoy him too much – he might take it upon himself to start exorcising anyway, and that was exactly what she wanted to avoid. "Never mind, don't answer that. I apologise for the inconvenience, but there should be a note on file at the Guild not to keep sending people out here. I don't need your help," she said.

"Don't need my help? Madam, if I told you what your neighbours had reported, you'd be appalled."

Stars, what had Granny done now? The next time she showed up, Abigail would tell her once and for all to stop meddling. "I promise you, it's nothing to do with me. If it's Jedrick Benson again, tell him his cat just *does* that sometimes."

"A Mrs Butcher was quite upset by a rude message left by the ghost," the wizard said, consulting a little book.

"Mrs Butcher is a prissy old windbag," Abigail retorted, which was quite true. Marjorie Butcher would be offended by a light breeze if it dared swish her skirts. "Wait, what did it say?"

The wizard paused. "I… don't feel it would be appropriate to tell you."

"Scrungenuts," said Granny, popping her head through the wall of the storeroom.

Abigail snorted, then slapped her hand over her mouth. She widened her eyes at Granny in a look that she hoped said "go away now, go away fast", but her meaning was obviously lost on the ghost, who let the rest of her translucent body drift through the wall, floating over to hover beside the wizard.

"He's a handsome one this time," she said smugly. "I knew they'd have to send a handsome one eventually. Don't you think he's handsome, Abbygirl?"

Abigail bit her lip to keep from laughing in disbelief. Yes, the wizard was handsome, but that was hardly important. The most beautiful lizards were the most venomous, after all, and a wizard on the lookout for a ghost was hardly any less dangerous for having sunny blond hair and cheekbones you could slice an apple on. Actually, now that she thought about it, she couldn't remember if she'd bought apples for Mr Stewart's tisane.

"This isn't funny, madam," said the wizard, and Abigail's attention snapped back to him. Oh, why did she have to get such a stickler this time? The last Guild wizard had been more than happy to take her word for it (and a pocket full of potions for his trouble) and slack off homewards. This one, handsome or not, looked terribly imposing. He held himself as if he anticipated an attack from any side, his posture humming with tension.

"No," said Abigail, straightening her face as much as she could. "Sorry." She had a wonderful lavender massage oil around here somewhere that would take all that tightness out of his shoulders – but no, he didn't seem the type.

"It is *quite* funny," said Granny. "It took me hours to get those stockings lined up. It's a long word, scrungenuts."

"Shush," hissed Abigail before she could stop herself. How was she supposed to get this wizard to believe there was no ghost if the ghost herself kept interrupting? On the plus side, from the way he was frowning at her, it didn't seem like he could see Granny. Small mercies.

"I will not shush!" said the wizard indignantly. "My apologies, Miss Hawthorne, but I really must insist. You will have to allow me to investigate the premises."

"Oh no I won't," said Abigail. "I have far too much to do to supervise you rootling around my home. You'll have to go back to the Guild and come another day. Preferably after the festival, when I don't have all these orders to complete." She indicated the order board, which was… empty? "Oh no, no, no," she cried, grabbing wildly at the tickets that littered the table. "They all fell down again."

"Sorry," said Granny. "I needed a pin to poke holes in Old Petey's curtains, and when I called one, they all came at once."

"Oh, why can't you just behave? Don't you have better things to do than bother me all the time?" Abigail snapped. The wizard's eyes widened in alarm at the anger in her voice. "Sorry, not you– I mean… Sorry."

"I'll be in my room, then," said Granny with a sniff, and blinked out of sight. Abigail suppressed a sigh.

"I don't, actually," said the wizard. "Have better things to do. It was this or bodyguard duty for the Prince of Alteria and between you and me, I'd give anything not to put the dress uniform on."

Was that… was he making a joke? She thought perhaps his lip was quirking a little. Maybe he wasn't as serious as he seemed. "Is it that ugly?" she asked.

"Two words," the wizard said. "Parti-coloured hose."

Granny popped her head through the ceiling above the wizard's head, and Abigail's laugh broke off into a squeak.

"Did someone say hose?" Granny asked with a grin.

Abigail scooped up an orange from the worktop – ah, now she remembered, she *had* been to the grocer – and threw it at Granny's face. She missed, and had to watch in shame as the orange sailed in a limp arc over the wizard's shoulder, landing somewhere out of sight. She'd have to remember to find it before it rotted. Granny cackled and vanished again; the wizard raised an eyebrow.

"There was a wasp," she said, and tried not to notice the amusement in his eyes. "Now, are you going to let me get on? I have a lot to do today."

“Certainly,” said the wizard, and sat down at the worktable.

“Um, no,” said the alchemist, wrinkling her freckled nose. “I meant that you should leave me to work.”

Cedric held his hands up and gave her his most innocent look. “I’m not stopping you. You carry on and I’ll just wait here and watch out for ghostly activity. When you’re done, you can show me the rest of the house, and if there’s no sign of any ghost, I’ll leave.”

She stared at him for a moment, then tutted and started clattering amongst the mess, gathering ingredients and tools. “Fine. Just don’t get in my way.”

“I’m Cedric, by the way,” he said. “Uh, Wizard Greene.” Kicking himself for the slip – they didn’t use titles in the office – he nudged a stack of books away from the edge of the table before they could topple.

“Abigail,” she said over her shoulder as she set a cauldron on the counter. “Hawthorne, as you know from the sign.”

Cedric wasn’t sure quite what was going on here, but as he watched the alchemist work, he realised that the chaos of the shop was likely entirely her doing. Abigail’s sleeves trailed into cauldrons no matter how many times she turned them up, and he got the impression that she could walk down the middle of an empty ballroom and still find something to knock over. She created clouds of detritus wherever she moved; an object, once it left her hand, seemed to cease to exist for her. Abigail mostly ignored him, humming to herself as she grated, chopped, and stirred, and Cedric couldn’t resist straightening out a few of the piles just for something to do. He designated an empty jug to hold spoons; he lined up the bottles in size order; he cleared a space and separated apples into two heaps, one red, one green. He was debating whether the apple he'd just found was more red or more green when Abigail swore quietly at the stove.

"Granny, can you pass me the ginger?" she said, holding out her hand without looking up.

Cedric spotted a ginger root under a stack of boxes; he wiggled it out, then crossed the room and placed it in Abigail's hand. As his fingers brushed hers, Abigail started violently, splashing a wave of green liquid onto the stove.

"Oh, sorry, I was a million miles away," she said over the sizzle. "Thanks. You didn't need to."

"Glad to help," Cedric smiled. "So you usually work with your grandmother?"

He'd only intended to make conversation, so he was surprised when a frown crept across her face and she dropped her gaze.

"Not anymore," she said, toying with the ginger. "Granny died a few months ago."

"I'm sorry. I didn't mean to upset you."

"No, no, it's fine, you couldn't have known. I'm just… I'm still not used to running the shop without her. I was only her assistant, you know, and I wasn't expecting to inherit for years." Abigail laughed, a little bitterly. "It's a lot to take in."

"Ah," said Cedric. "That explains…" He waved his hand at the rest of the shop.

“It’s not always like this,” she said, sounding defensive. “I’m perfectly capable. It’s because of the festival. There are too many orders to keep track of, and I’ve only got one pair of hands.”

“Of course,” said Cedric. “Couldn’t you hire help for the festival?”

“Oh no, that would be worse! There’s a system, you see. Someone new would just get confused. I just need to work a bit harder and I’ll be fine.”

“There’s a *system*?” Cedric couldn’t imagine anything that looked less like a system than the current state of Hawthorne and Daughters.

Her glare was icy. “Of course there is. Granny had a place for everything, as long as you know where to look. She’s always telling me to pay more attention to where I put things.” She stopped herself and gave another little laugh. “I mean, she was, of course. She doesn’t any more. How could she?”

Cedric smiled gently; her grief was obviously still raw. He suspected she’d hardly had time to catch her breath, let alone process her loss. “Well, while I’m here, why don’t I give you a hand? I might not know the system, but I can chop things, and I tie a pretty neat bow.”

“No, that’s–” Abigail looked like she was warring with herself. “Actually, that would be great. Thank you. Can you stir this clockwise while I try and find the apples? I’m sure I bought some, but I don’t know where they’ve got to since then.”

Cedric took the spoon she offered and set to stirring, grinning in anticipation of the moment she realised what he'd done.

"Oh!"

She'd spotted them. He turned to see her staring at him in disbelief, holding an apple in each hand.

"You tidied up?" she asked.

"I couldn't resist," he said. "Sorry if I ruined the system. I didn't move anything far."

Abigail shook her head. "No, this is useful. Thank you." She smiled at him, a sunny, genuine smile, and Cedric's chest did that weird tightening thing again. Maybe he needed to visit the healer for a check up once he was back at the Guild.

"Well then," he grinned back. "Let's get to work."

After some protest, Abigail agreed to flip the shop sign to 'closed' and lock the door so they'd have some breathing space to tackle the existing orders. The afternoon slid away into evening as they worked, Abigail fluttering around the workroom in a distracted but determined fashion, Cedric slicing and stirring and lifting forgotten pans off the stove before they could boil over. The way they moved around each other reminded him of a dance: several times he dragged furniture out of her way just before she crashed into it, and more than once she held her hand out for an ingredient he'd just picked up. When it got too dark to read the labels on the jars, he flicked charmlight into the corners of the room; Abigail didn't even bat an eyelid, she was so focused on her work.

"Sneeze drops, sneeze drops, where would they… no, wait, I know." She rummaged in a drawer that bristled with knives until she found a small jar and held it up triumphantly. “Of course!”

“Of course,” echoed Cedric sarcastically. “Why wouldn’t they be tucked away over there rather than shelved with the rest of the cold remedies?”

“Because,” Abigail said, “the knife grinder’s boy was prone to sneezing fits when he was little, so it was easier to keep them where he could get hold of them himself.”

“And how old is the knife grinder’s boy now?”

“…forty-six.” Abigail laughed. “But Granny still calls – called – him boy.”

Cedric chuckled. The amount of time she must have wasted looking for everything, if it was stored based on someone else’s memories… “You know, you could make your own system.”

“What’s wrong with the system I have? It worked for Granny for fifty years.”

“That’s exactly my point. It’s your grandmother’s system. Not yours. Wouldn’t it be easier to keep the place straight if you put things where they made sense to *you*?” He stopped. Abigail was looking at him with a strange expression on her face. “What?”

“It really bothers you, doesn’t it? The mess?” she said.

“I– Everything is easier when things are tidy,” he said, taken aback.

“That, I will grant you,” she said. “Fine. Can you do something about the herb storage? Gather them all here by the stove, and put them in some kind of order?”

“Alphabetical or by use?” he asked, and she snorted and threw a dishcloth at his head. He caught it, laughing, and started looking for the comfrey.

Slowly the teetering piles of chaos began to transform into something resembling a working alchemist's shop. Cedric pinned an order ticket to each completed basket and placed them by the door, ready to be delivered the next day. His back clicked as he set down a basket filled with a rather alarming assortment of attraction charms for someone named "Old Petey", and he stretched widely as he walked back to the kitchen.

"Tell me there's not much more to do," he groaned. "I didn't realise you were going to work me like a carthorse."

"You volunteered," said Abigail with a snort. "But I think that was the last one."

"Really?"

"Well, there's probably something I missed – there always is – but honestly, I'm too tired to care." She flopped down onto a stool and dropped her forehead onto the tabletop. A spoon clattered to the floor.

Cedric sat down next to her, and had the ridiculous urge to smooth her hair back where it had escaped from her braid and lay wildly against the marble. He clenched his twitching fingers, and said instead, "You did a good job." She might be messy, but she was clearly talented. He hadn't even been able to name half those potions, let alone known the recipes by heart.

"Ugh," she muttered into the table. "I mean, thanks. I couldn't have done it without you."

"You'd have managed," he said, resting his head next to hers on the cool surface. "Might have taken longer, though."

She rolled her head to the side and looked at him sleepily. "You have jam on your face."

"So do you." This time he couldn't stop his hand; he just watched as his thumb swept the smear from her cheek. Did her eyes flutter closed at his touch, or was she just dropping off? The thought made him realise how unprofessional he was being.

"I should get back to the Guild," Cedric made himself say. He got up so fast the stool keeled over, but he made himself ignore it, grabbed his cloak from the display rack he'd draped it on, and settled it around his shoulders.

"Oh, yes, of course." Abigail said, sitting up abruptly. "You're satisfied there's no ghost?"

Oh, right, the ghost. He'd almost forgotten. "No, I'm afraid I'll still need to investigate that." His voice sounded absurdly formal, and he winced. "I'll need to come back tomorrow. I'll just find an inn for tonight."

"Stars, don't be ridiculous," she said. "It's the night before the spring festival. You think there's a single room or barn out there that hasn't been booked for weeks? Jedrick Benson lets out his greenhouse, even, and there'll be six or seven people squashed in there among the seedlings."

"Oh." She was right. "Well, I'll just camp somewhere." It would be uncomfortable, but he wasn't going back to the Guild without this ghost problem being fully resolved; the field team would be desperate to poke holes in his performance, and he'd already wasted a day.

"Come on," she said, laughing around a yawn. "I'm not that cruel. You can stay in the spare room."

The groan Abigail made as she sank onto her bed was so loud she even startled herself. She didn't think she'd *ever* been this tired. Her eyes drifted closed, and she considered just lying down as she was and letting the exhaustion take her, but the sleeves of her dress were unpleasantly damp, and she knew if she didn't dismantle what was left of her braid, her hair would be one enormous knot in the morning. Besides, it was like Granny always said…

"Square up at night, wake up just right!" It took Abigail a moment to realise that Granny's cheery voice wasn't just in her head. When she opened her eyes, Granny beamed back at her. "You worked hard today, Abbygirl. I'm proud of you – don't you roll your eyes at me, girl. Come on, get yourself sorted."

"I'm sorry I lost my temper earlier,' Abigail said as she undressed and began to set herself to rights. "It was all just a bit much, with the wizard showing up and all those orders to make."

"Psh. What's a lobbed orange among family? I'm sure I've thrown worse at you – and with better aim. Anyway, the wizard was helpful in the end, wasn't he? He's much nicer than the last one."

"He is," she admitted. "Though that isn't hard."

Granny grinned. "Seemed like a bit more than him not being a toad-faced git. Seemed like you got on well."

"Ye-es…" Abigail paused with her hairbrush

hovering mid-stroke. Granny seemed oddly calm about the presence of a ghost-hunting wizard. "You have to be careful, though, until he leaves tomorrow. You can't keep popping in and out or he'll get suspicious and then…" She didn't want to say it. She didn't even want to think about Granny being gone.

"I'll be as quiet as a mouse," said Granny, chuckling. "Unless I need to help with something."

"Granny, no! Leave him alone, please. When I said goodnight he was unpacking all sorts of wizard kit – he might have something in there that could really hurt you." Abigail yawned. Finally done with her ablutions – and feeling better for it – she slipped on her nightgown and let herself fall into bed. "Plus, he's probably as exhausted as I am. You should let him sleep," she mumbled.

"Oh, so you really are planning on sleeping tonight?" Granny asked wickedly. "Shame. I thought this one seemed promising."

"Ugh." Abigail sat up. "You're not still on at me to find a boyfriend, are you?"

"Boyfriend, lover, whatever. I thought a wizard would be a good fit for you – a nice educated boy. Not many in town, though, so it's a good thing the Guild ignored that letter you wrote and sent this Cedric fellow out anyway."

"Granny." Abigail was fully awake now, and she put as much warning into her tone as she could muster. "*Please* tell me you haven't been terrorising the neighbours just to get the Wizard's Guild to send out men for me to meet."

Granny pursed her lips. "I can't tell you that."

"Stars, Granny! You can't do that!" Abigail shouted, and threw her pillow at the ghost; Granny winked out of existence and there was a loud clatter as the pillow knocked everything off the dresser.

Moments later, the door slammed open and Cedric charged in, brandishing a wand and a silver bottle. He'd have been the very image of an imposing wizard… if he'd had time to put on any clothes.

"Abigail, are you okay?" he asked. "Is it the ghost?"

Every thought had gone out of Abigail's head. She could only stare at him. She'd already thought he was handsome, but if his hair had reminded her of sunlight, she'd need a whole summer's worth of sunny days to describe how his body made her feel.

"There was shouting?" he said, sounding somewhat less confident. "And a big bang?" He lowered his wand, and her eyes travelled down with it.

No, thank the stars, he was in fact wearing something… though that something was *very* brief. And embroidered with little constellations – was that the Crowned Serpent? Cedric cleared his throat. Abigail felt a hot rush of embarrassment flood her from head to toe as she realised she was still staring, and snapped her gaze up to meet his. He quirked an eyebrow.

"I'm sorry," she said. "I didn't mean to look – I mean, I didn't mean to wake you. I had a bad dream."

"And the ghost?"

"There's no ghost."

Cedric sighed. "If you say so. I take it you're not in imminent peril?" he asked.

Abigail shook her head. “I’m fine.”

“And… you’ve seen enough of this?” he said, waving a hand at his torso.

She didn’t trust her voice. She felt the insane desire to grab that hand and pull him into her arms and feel that sunshiney warmth against her – but no. She couldn’t. She had to think about Granny. She pressed her lips together and nodded.

“Then I’m going back to bed,” he said. Was she imagining it, or did he sound disappointed?

“Goodnight,” said Abigail as the door swung shut. She hoped Cedric would find it easier to sleep than she would; tired as she was, she had rather a lot to think about now.

“Girls these days,” tutted Granny from the eaves. “No initiative.”

Cedric was not looking forward to Abigail waking up, partly because thinking about the previous night made his stomach knot up with embarrassment, but also because he didn’t think she was going to be very happy with what he’d discovered when he came into the workroom that morning. He pushed his worry into busyness, as he always did, and was tidying the cauldron cupboard when she finally joined him in the workroom.

“Do you really need three of the tiny little ones?” he said by way of greeting.

“Yes,” she replied without even looking at him. “Wow, it looks great in here. I haven’t seen so much space in weeks.” She did a little spin in the newly-open space, knocking over a small end-table.

Cedric snorted. "I see my work will not be long-lasting."

"Oh, shut up. What's this?" she asked, poking one of the boxes he'd placed on the worktop.

"Sweet buns, from the bakery down the road. Um, I didn't know where to find any breakfast things. I did make this, though," he said, handing her a steaming cup of tea.

"Oh, you're a lifesaver." She took a huge gulp, then winced. "Hot."

"Listen, I'm sorry about last night," he said. Better to get the conversation over with. "Bursting into your room like that. You, um, didn't need to see that."

She groaned and went pink. "Stars, no, it should be me apologising. You were just trying to do your job. I shouldn't have been staring but I couldn't–" She slapped a hand over her mouth. "Ugh. I'm sorry."

Cedric couldn't suppress his smile. She was clearly as flustered by the encounter as he was. "Shall we just agree to change the subject?"

"*Please*," she said.

"All right," he said with a shrug. "Good buns?"

Abigail spluttered. "You said you were changing the subject!"

"The breakfast buns," he clarified, laughing. Oh, it was a terrible joke, but worth it to see her blush deepen even further.

"You– *Oh*. Yes. Breakfast buns. *Those* buns are very nice and also the only thing under discussion," she said carefully. "Are there more in there?" She pointed at the other box.

"Ah," he said. "No, that's less fun." He tilted the box towards her, and watched her face fall as she took in the dozens of order requests inside. "These were all on the doormat this morning."

Abigail spat a curse that would have made Cedric's casebook blush. "Oh, this stars-damned town! I'm *never* going to be finished in time. And I wanted to buy some gifts before tonight's feast – well, that doesn't matter now, because I'm not even going to get to *go* to the feast, all because George bloody Plum can't remember he's allergic to beans–"

"Hey, hey, hey," said Cedric, taking the cup back before she could slosh hot tea over them both. "There's not so many orders here. We can handle this."

"We?" She rounded on him. "Don't you have ghost-hunting to do?"

"It can wait," he said. He kept forgetting about the ghost; the only bearer of chaos he'd seen any sign of was one clumsy, over-worked alchemist. Maybe Jedrick Benson's cat really did just do that, and Marjorie Butcher had an overactive imagination and a sailor's vocabulary. "Come on, have the last bun, and I'll take a look at these."

For a moment, he thought she was going to argue, but eventually she nodded and pulled the bakery box towards her; Cedric started reading through the orders, sorting them into two tidy stacks.

"Okay," he said. "These ones we can fill from what we made yesterday, including George Plum's medicine."

"And those?"

"Can wait until after the festival." When Abigail began to protest, he held up a hand. "I think you've got so hung up on keeping things running that you've forgotten you're allowed a day off as much as anyone else is."

Her shoulders sagged. "Fine. But I'll want to read them myself to be sure."

"I'll put them on the board," he grinned. "Right, first order – you ready?"

Cedric was struck once again by how well the two of them worked together, especially now it didn't take a wild scramble to find every new ingredient. They lined the baskets up with the other completed orders just in time for the arrival of the delivery boys, who goggled at the sheer number of items but valiantly loaded them all into their cart.

As the cart clattered away, Abigail whooped and seized Cedric in a hug. It took a moment to convince his body he wasn't under attack; before he had a chance to return the embrace, she'd already let him go, apologising, and he kicked himself.

"You're tenser than I am, and that's saying something!" she laughed. "Hang on, I've got a great recipe for a relaxing oil so you can give those shoulders a break – I'll whip some up now, call it a thank you for your help. You just sort of rub it in after a bath, though sometimes you need to get someone else to do the bits you can't reach."

"You're supposed to be taking the day off," he said, to deflect from the entirely distracting images her words had painted in his mind.

"Stars, a day off. I won't even know what to do with myself." She beamed at him; this time, when the thump in his chest came, he was almost expecting it.

"I have an idea," said Cedric, before he could talk himself out of it. To hell with the Guild's propriety. "Would you like to go to the festival?"

"Well, yes," laughed Abigail. "That was the plan all along."

He could feel the heat rising to his cheeks. "No, I mean – would you like to go to the festival with me?"

Oh, scrungenuts.

"Cedric, I can't," she said, even as Granny burst through the ceiling shouting, "Yes!"

Abigail glared at the ghost, then returned her gaze to Cedric, whose smile had fallen.

"What do you mean, you can't?" screeched Granny. "You like him, he likes you, go!!"

"Are you having second thoughts about the shop?" he asked. "I promise, the world won't stop because Abigail Hawthorne takes the afternoon off."

"No, it's not that. It's… I can't go with *you*." Abigail winced as she saw her words strike home.

Cedric stiffened, and his voice took on that formal tone she'd begun to think of as his Professional Wizard voice. "I see. I apologise for mistaking your interest. It was inappropriate of me to ask."

"No, no, you didn't mistake anything. Listen, I would love to go with you, but–" There was nothing for it; she was going to have to explain everything. "I haven't been entirely truthful with you. There is a ghost, and that's why I can't…"

"The ghost threatens you if you try to leave? Why didn't you say something? That's what I'm here for, I can exorcise it–" He started fiddling with the equipment on his belt.

"I don't *want* you to exorcise her!"

The shout left her breathless. Cedric stopped trying to unhook his wand, and simply stared at her.

"It's your grandmother, isn't it?" he said, and when she nodded, not trusting her voice, he put a gentle hand on her shoulder. "I'm sorry. I didn't even think."

"You can't exorcise her," Abigail whispered, and was relieved when he nodded. The relief didn't last long, however; she flinched back in shock as Granny's translucent face popped up in front of Cedric's.

"Abigail Juniper Hawthorne, what's all this nonsense? I've never said anything about stopping you from dating. Stars, I've been trying to *get* you to date."

"I know!" Abigail said, "At the expense of the neighbours' sanity, and don't think we won't have words about that. But I don't have time to date, when I'm looking after the shop, and more importantly, I don't *want* to date if it means I lose you!"

Granny looked horrified. "Why on earth would it mean you'd lose me?"

"Is that her? Are you talking to her now?" said Cedric, looking wildly around the room. Abigail held up a forestalling hand; so did Granny, for all the use it was.

"Sorry," said Cedric. "I'll, um. I'll make some tea."

Abigail turned back to Granny, who repeated, "Why would you lose me, sweetheart?"

Abigail felt tears prick her eyes. "Well, this is your unfinished business, isn't it? This is why you're still, you know, a ghost. You said it last night, you want me to find a boyfriend, but I know how it goes. If I do, you'll be all fulfilled and disappear and I'll be all alone… What? Why are you laughing?"

Granny was cackling so hard her body was drifting up towards the ceiling. "Abbygirl, I love you, but really? You think *that's* the only thing holding me here? Oh, you look so serious!" Granny floated down and laid a ghostly hand over Abigail's cheek. "I promise you, there's a lot more going on in my afterlife than fixing my granddaughter's love life."

"Oh," said Abigail, feeling very small.

"I want you to be happy, sweetheart, and I want you to fall in love if you want to. But I also want the shop to succeed. I want your mother to sell her paintings, and your brother to have more kids. I want to scare the living daylights out of that rascal Petey for throwing me over when I was seventeen. I've got a lot of unfinished business, Abbygirl, and none of it means you can't live your life."

"Oh," Abigail said again. She swiped at her wet cheeks. "I just thought–"

"You think too much, trust me. Makes a good alchemist, but a wrinkly one," Granny said, pointing at her own face, and Abigail smiled through her tears. "There, that's a smile. Now, go and tell that nice boy to stop polishing that teacup before he takes the pattern off. Go on your date, and don't you worry about me, girl, I'll be here when you get back – no, wait, I'll be here tomorrow. Give you and your young man some space." She gave a wicked grin. "Be a shame to waste those buns."

"Granny!" Abigail gasped, but the ghost had already vanished.

"Tea?" said Cedric, as Abigail slumped down at the table.

"Stars, yes," she said. "I'm sorry for… well, all of that, really. This probably isn't the kind of case you were expecting."

Cedric chuckled. "You'd be surprised. But you're okay?"

"Yes," Abigail said, wiping her face on her apron. "Yes, I think I am. Listen, I need to ask you something."

"About ghosts?"

"No, forget ghosts. Somehow I don't think there'll be any more issues. Is your offer still open? Turns out I have a day off, no particular obligations to any spectral relatives, and a handsome wizard standing in my shop who I'd very much like to show around the festival."

The sun was high in the sky before Cedric finally managed to get Abigail out of the shop; every time she moved towards the door it sparked another round of "sorry, I'll just sort…" and "one minute, let me quickly…". Eventually, laughing, he simply grabbed her hand, removed the pot she'd just placed onto the stove, and physically dragged her outside before she could protest.

She blinked at him, then burst into laughter of her own. "Sorry, sorry, I get a bit–"

"Distracted?" He raised an amused eyebrow as they spoke the final word together. "Believe me, I'm rapidly getting used to it. But don't worry – for the rest of the day, I plan to be a pretty good distraction myself."

When he shut the door behind them, he took a great satisfaction in twisting the shop sign firmly to 'closed'.

Adie Hart is a lover of stories and the words behind them. With a background in the history and literature of the Ancient World, and an abiding love of classic fairy tales, she writes everything from fun fantasy adventures to dark mythological retellings.

Reviews

Editor's Pick

The Secret Casebook of Simon Feximal by KJ Charles

Robert Caldwell has served as the companion to the ghost-hunter and paranormal investigator Simon Feximal for twenty years, publishing fictionalised versions of his cases to wild acclaim. Now, with the dangers of the First World War looming, he feels it is finally time to reveal the truth behind his relationship with Feximal, in a no-holds-barred memoir to be published only after his death. This is not exactly a novel, but a collection of shorter stories, presented as different cases Feximal and Caldwell investigate, that build into a full arc; you could dip into them as standalone short stories if you really wanted, but for the true emotional payoff I recommend reading from beginning to end.

It does, as you might expect from the set up, owe something to Sherlock Holmes, but though we have a genius, oddball detective and his more practical assistant-cum-chronicler as our leads, the story swiftly becomes its own. One of the strengths in all of Charles's work is the wonderful knack she has for writing characters who may seem prickly and unapproachable, but who compel you to peel back their layers and find out what makes them the way they are. Feximal and Caldwell are no exception to this – I found both of them fascinating characters, full of depth, and I loved how they developed both individually and as a couple.

The stories walk the line between horror, fantasy, and romance in a way that feels pretty unique in my reading experience. I'm not generally someone who enjoys horror, but this worked well for me, I think because the genuinely creepy elements are mixed with a wonderful thread of dark humour and that classic mystery feel. The paranormal scenes are incredibly tense, but not particularly gory or graphic, so horror wusses like me should just about be okay – but maybe keep the lights on… There's a great list of content warnings on the author's site if you want to check them out before you read.

As you would expect if you've read any of KJ Charles's work previously, this book is steamy, pretty much from the get-go. The first time Caldwell meets Feximal, they're seized in the grip of a ghost whose unfinished business is, well, getting down to business, which leads to a somewhat unorthodox method of exorcism. It might sound like the set up for mindless erotica, but there's much more to it than that – there's a real focus on consent and communication that keeps it firmly in a darkly romantic vein, and the character work is so exquisite that every sex scene serves a purpose in both the plot and the development of the leads' relationship. It's definitely an adult read, but as much because of the darkness and depth of the characters' world views as because of the sexual content.

I'm a big fan of Charles, but something I love about this book in particular is the world building and the way it is shown. We only get glimpses of the world as they come up in the context of each case, but this is a very clever historical fantasy. Sometimes with urban fantasy, modern or historical, the changes made to the world are only superficial, but here there's a genuine feel that the differences run through society all the way to the core. The real world Victorian obsession with the occult definitely helps with the feel of this, but there are numerous small touches throughout that really make the world come alive – and I really thought that Caldwell's narration, writing in hindsight in 1914 about cases from the turn of the century, added wonderfully to this. There's a sense of irony and pathos to stories told after the fact that just adds more texture to the world.

I could read dozens more books in this series if they existed. If you love this and are looking for more, *Spectred Isle* takes place in the same world with tangentially related characters, but I also recommend Charles's Regency fantasy series, which begins with *The Magpie Lord.* All in all, this is a must-read if you like your fantasy dark, historical, and sexy.

<u>About the author</u>: After twenty years in UK publishing including a stint at Mills & Boon, KJ Charles is now a full-time writer. She lives in London with her husband, two kids, an out-of-control garden and an increasingly murderous cat.

<u>About the reviewer</u>: Asha is the Indie Bites Review Editor. She is also a book blogger with a life-long love of fantasy and a towering TBR.

I Belong to the Earth by JA Ironside

Review by Laura Laakso, author of Fallible Justice

For someone who isn't that into YA, I've been reading an awful lot of it recently. *I Belong to the Earth* has been, by far, the most enjoyable book in the genre I've read for quite some time. In fact, it's probably been the most enjoyable book I've read this year.

I first came across the *Unveiled* series in the *Dissecting Dragons* speculative fiction podcast co-hosted by Ironside. What I heard about the books and the main character intrigued me enough that I thought I had better get the first book, and I'm glad I did. The genre is a mixture of urban fantasy and gothic ghost story. I had some reservations about the latter aspects ahead of delving in because I'm not a big fan of horror, but that said, the paranormal elements never made me feel uncomfortable and the story got me so hooked I kept forgetting to go to bed.

In the book, Emlyn and her family move to a village in the Yorkshire moors following the death of her mother in a car accident that nearly killed Emlyn and her younger sister, Amy. Each family member has a different way of dealing with the trauma, but Emlyn's life is complicated by the fact that she can see the Dead. Her older sister Grace is soon drawn into the Pattern; a tragic love story that repeats in the moors and has claimed the lives of countless girls of the decades and centuries. Only Emlyn has the power to unravel the Pattern and break the cycle of death and misery.

Given the dark setting, it would have been easy to allow the characters to become caricatures of angst and brooding, but I felt Ironside struck a careful balance between portraying the world through the eyes of a traumatised teenager and keeping her relatable. Initially I thought Grace was just a little too mean, but much of this is explained as the story progresses and all the sisters' relationships with one another came to a satisfactory conclusion by the end. It isn't all hugs and puppies, but relationships rarely are. I also felt that throughout the story, the girls' father was a little too absent, but again there is an explanation for it. Of the supporting characters, Mrs Cranford was my absolute favourite, but I do have a soft spot for older women with agency and independent agenda, so I was already predisposed to love her.

The paranormal and ghostly elements were finely woven through the more mundane aspects of Emlyn's life. I guessed quite early on that the Pattern reached further than Emlyn appreciated, but that is in part because I read like a writer rather than a reader! Still, the fact that I guessed right on several occasions in no detracted from my enjoyment of the story.

Overall, *I Belong to the Earth* is a fine book that I would recommend to anyone who likes the YA and urban fantasy genres. I will definitely be getting the second book in the series and will look out for the various novellas as well.

<u>About the author</u>: J. A. Ironside (Jules) grew up in a house full of books in rural Dorset. She mostly writes fantasy and sci-fi, for both adults and YA. Often this leans towards the dark fantastic. Her favourite things include books (obviously), slippers, cheese and surreal conversations.

<u>About the reviewer</u>: Laura is a Finn, who has spent most of her adult life in England. She is currently living in Hertfordshire with her two dogs. When she is not writing, editing or plotting, she works as an accountant. With two degrees in archaeology, she possesses useful skills for disposing of or digging up bodies, and if her

internet search history is anything to go by, she is on several international watch lists.

Haze by Rebecca Crunden
Review by Josie Jaffrey, author of May Day

Haze launches us into a story that starts off brightly: Erik and Eliza have just got engaged. At nineteen, they're young, but Eliza's family loves Erik almost as much as she does, even if the small town of Riverside has never trusted him. You see, Erik's father is a murderer. He killed Erik's mother when Erik was still a boy, and the townspeople assume: like father, like son. Eliza has always brushed off their nonsense as simple prejudice, until she gets a call from Erik's ex-girlfriend, warning her that Erik is not all that he seems. She wants them to meet in person. Against her better instincts, Eliza is inclined to do as the girl asks, until Erik tells her something that chills her to the bone: his ex is dead. She has been for five years.

Having read a few of Crunden's short stories in the past, I thought I knew what I was getting into with this supernatural novel. I assumed it would be sweet and romantic, with probably a bit of dark ghosty stuff thrown in, but nothing too intense. I was so very wrong, in the best way.

Haze is a dark book. It quickly becomes apparent that Riverside is not all it seems. Without getting too spoilery, I'll say that it isn't just a fun mountain town where people go hiking in the forest and enjoy riding horses on the ranch. It's somewhere that people can easily fall between the cracks, particularly if they're trying to forget about the demons that are haunting them. There's always someone willing to sell you something that will take the pain away, and none of them have your best interests at heart. But – and this was probably my very favourite thing about the book – none of these people are caricatures. There's structure to what they do. They have depth. They care, they strive, they make terrible, terrible decisions. However much you might want to hate them, and however much some of the other characters might hate them, they are presented as real, fully-formed people in a way that makes it difficult not to have some sympathy for them. In Riverside, everyone is struggling, and they do what they can.

After a terrible accident changes her life and forces her and Erik apart, Eliza struggles more than most. She is about as far from the goody-goody heroine archetype that it's possible to get, and yet you are rooting for her every step of the way. Crunden doesn't flinch from recounting the heart-wrenching cycle that ensues, and Eliza's inability to break it. Instead, the author lets her characters feel their grief in all its forms, without judgement. That really resonated with me in these difficult times. Supported by subplots of addiction and violence, the picture painted is bleak, but never grotesque. It's a difficult line to walk, but in this novel the feeling of hopelessness it creates is a wonderful portrait of a failing town and a great counterbalance to the main plot. Which is, of course, a hopeful one.

At its heart, despite its darkness, *Haze* is a love story, a proper romance. The question is: can Eliza and Erik somehow find their way back to the great love of their lives, despite the huge obstacles in their way? And wow, are there obstacles, both natural and supernatural. Beyond those I've discussed above, there are several terrible events that result in ghostly interventions, all of which conspire to keep the couple apart. The mystery, which the story unfurls beautifully over the course of the book, is: why? And what is wrong with Erik anyway?

You'll have to read the book yourself to find out.

About the author: Rebecca Crunden is an indie author of fantasy, science fiction and romance who lives in Cork, Ireland.

About the reviewer: Josie Jaffrey is an indie author of urban fantasy, paranormal romance and young adult fantasy who lives in Oxford, England.

Printed in Great Britain
by Amazon

76564358R00087